THE
Lavender

Theory of Personal
Contentment
and other musings

JUDE DOWNES

Jude Downes is an Australian poet and story-weaver of metaphoric stories for healing and life's journey. She is an author, a Clairvoyant and Intuitive Mentor. Jude's healing words work with metaphors through the power of story to affect deep and lasting transformation. She is passionate about helping others on their life journey.

Her creative writing is born of living a country life in a quaint cottage with a lovely garden along with her husband and cat. Kangaroos and wombats are part of her daily life as she ventures out to write in her Dreaming Studio overlooking a standing stone circle and the mountains beyond.

Jude is a 'Healer with Words'. She encourages people to write a new chapter in their personal life story. She is the creator of sacred workshops and retreats. Her intimate connection with the Goddess ~ the Earth Mother and the messages that come from nature weave a path in the unity between mind, body, soul and emotions to form the foundation of her business, Dreaming the Seed.

www.judedownes.com

For Mum

First published 2024

A self published title designed and produced
by Adala Publishing
www.adalapublishing.com.au

 A catalogue record for this
book is available from the
National Library of Australia

ISBN 978-0-6453485-2-1 (Print)
ISBN 978-0-6453485-3-8 (eBook)
ISBN 978-0-6453485-4-5 (PDF)

www.judedownes.com

Contents

Introduction

This little book started life with a working title of *The Lavender Theory of Personal Contentment and other musings* and it stuck. It's a book of metaphors for the journey of life written through poems, affirmations and short stories.

There is magic within the words, and vibrations that are feel-good in nature. That's intentional!

The only connection to lavender (as per the title) is that it is a generational plant loved by the women in my family back to my Great Grandmother. When I asked my guides what I should call my book, this was the name that immediately dropped into my conscious thoughts. Perhaps it is a message directly from my ancestor.

It is definitely *not* a book about lavender. However, one of the stories written is about how lavender plants and their flowers can help us navigate strange pathways. It's a quirky title for a quirky book by a quirky Crone. A Crone's view of the world is through a different lens when she has lived a life of many stories, with more to come.

I have written since I was at primary school (a long time ago with a break for life's ups and downs in between). I began writing again almost thirty years ago and I haven't looked back. Now feels like the right time to publish this work, as I just keep writing more poems and more stories!

When we create something in life we love, it feels like a fabulous opportunity to share once we overcome the fear of rejection and doubt over 'is it good enough'. In this chaos-driven world, who knows how much our words or art or flowers or cake baking might bring love and understanding to others navigating this wacky life. My words are a pin drop in the grand scheme of things. They're a tender touch that shines through in this book as the metaphors bring in those aha moments.

It is my understanding of the lavender connection in one of the stories that touches the soul gently, just by being the generous, calming protective influence she is.

Every story is a picture to me. I write what I am shown visually just mere moments after I see the image in my heart and mind. I love that! I rarely make many changes, as it truly just flows from my heart to the hearts of whoever reads my words. That's enough for me.

The *Lavender Theory of Personal Contentment and other musings* is designed to offer stories as metaphors for life. It's a way of viewing life through storytelling. I learned a long time ago that stories are a big part of our healing commitment. They are ways of seeing life with a different view to healing and wellbeing.

Each story is an immersion into being part of the journey of words. Or they can offer themselves up as meditations where you might see yourself or someone close to you through a different viewfinder. In understanding self, our take-away will be something profound.

Each poem also offers my unique view of the world. Some are free verse poems (without rhyme) and others are rhyming. All flowed with love for what I was writing at the time.

Many of the writings are of a mystical, magical nature and the wisdom of the feminine spirit is strong within many of them. I personally see the magic that overlays our everyday world. I see beyond the ordinary into the world of the extraordinary at times. Often, the mystical and magical make the best metaphors!

Rather than write what *I* feel are the meanings behind each metaphor, I am drawn to offer you, the reader an opportunity to see how a story or poem fits with your own understanding. Most often, it is in the reading and an 'ahhh I get it', rather than attempting to work it out logically that offers the most meaning to each of us. This is how story touches us in our heart and soul. The deeper understanding takes place within us.

It is my hope that my stories and poems offer you a lifeline on your own journey, or as simply a place of enjoyment; reading them over a morning cup of tea, perhaps.

All my words come from a place of magic within me, where words become the creative spoke in my unique wheel of life. As I look at the vision of how they are created, it is a series of words in a jumble until I begin to write, and the words begin to form sentences and paragraphs until there is a whole story written down.

Words I write have offered me a healing journey in times of pain and times of hurt. They've offered me time to be in a space of writing at frantic speed as the words chose to be expressed in any given moment. It's a process that is my own way of working. Out of word chaos, a short story or poem is born. I love that!

It's my way. So, enjoy the journey of words in *The Lavender Theory of Personal Contentment and other musings*. I enjoyed writing every single one of them.

With Love

Jude xx

Eat Chocolate Cake

Dance in the moonlight; sing loudly in the rain
Do cartwheels at sunrise; let the colours keep you sane
Eat ice-cream for breakfast and chocolate cake too
This world's far too serious to be so blue

Chant a new song; wear boho with pride
Life's too short; let your heart be your guide
Get up to mischief; let's see your humorous side
These changes we bring will not be denied

Open a door and yes, the window too
The winds of change are bringing a new view
Circle the wagons; we fight for our freedom
The key is in joy; not in life's museum

Laugh outrageously; don't keep it in
Because the bastards will tell you… laughter is a sin
It's a brand-new world; we know it well
But unless we live it; there will never be a groundswell

Take a bite of simplicity by challenging the old
It might just make time to turn dust into gold
Dance up that storm; clear the bloody decks
Because something fabulous, is coming to us next!

Don't wait your turn; take the chance on you now
There's no time to waste; just show the world how!!!!

Tapestry of Sisterhood

A few short years ago, a young woman was in the late stages of her pregnancy. Her partner worked long hours in order to make ends meet. She sat at home alone day after day, crying softly to herself that circumstances had led her away from her family and friends.

This young woman's mother lived a thousand miles away and so too did her dearest friends. Women she called sisters regardless of their individual relationships.

Since they moved house to be closer to her partner's work, she hadn't the courage to go out and make new friends. When her partner came home from work, he was too exhausted to talk much. They struggled to communicate with each other because they didn't know what to say to ease the feelings of despair. The man knew his partner was lonely, but felt powerless to help, and soon they stopped talking altogether.

The woman longed for her sisterhood of family and friends. She longed for the women with whom she had woven a tapestry of experiences in her life thus far.

One glorious day, the woman awoke with a renewed sense of hope. She placed her hands on her swelling tummy and whispered to the baby – 'it's going to be alright, baby. We are going to be just fine. I know your dad works long hours so that we can live and eat and I know that right now we have to spend so much time by ourselves, but baby, I just know that a miracle is about to happen. I don't know what it is, but we have to have faith'.

The young woman began to prepare the house for their imminent and joyous new arrival. She decided to make the house a home for her little family. She was so convinced that her miracle was about to appear, that she began smiling again and singing to her baby the lullabies of her childhood.

The young woman's husband came home from work and noticed that his partner seemed happier than she had in the preceding months since they moved. When he asked if something special had happened, she opened her heart and soul to him and told him of her loneliness and that she missed her friends and family. She told him that just that day, a deep inner knowing had awakened within her core that everything was going to be fine.

He breathed a sigh of relief. He had thought he was losing his precious family but seeing his partner looking so radiant and content he felt his own heart open more than ever before. He wanted to protect them and do everything in his power to ensure that they were safe and loved.

The next day, he secretly made a few phone calls to some very special people. He had also noticed other young mothers in the street where they lived, as well as some older women who may offer the wisdom of the elder, when her mum wasn't around. He spoke to them and invited them to meet his partner.

One very special Saturday, close to the time of their baby's birth, there was a knock at the door. The man looked at his partner and said, 'why don't you get that, love'. The woman thought it strange that he would ask this of her when she was so heavily pregnant and moving about was an effort. She went to the door anyway. When the young woman opened the door, standing there were the most beautiful faces she had ever seen.

Her mother and dearest friends were standing there on her very own doorstep. There were some unfamiliar faces as well. Faces she would come to know and love.

Each woman had a gift in her hands. Gifts so special, that she would remember each and every woman long after they had returned to their homes.

The women had been in touch with one another and created a tapestry of their journey together. Some had just begun the tapestry, while others had filled their spaces entirely and were beginning new ones. When her sisterhood of family and friends were no longer there, all the young woman needed to do was feel the love woven into the tapestry of their interwoven lives. She would always be close to her sisters, no matter where they lived.

Her partner stood quietly in the doorway and saw the love on her face as she embraced each and every one of her sisters. He knew they would survive anything as long as he remembered the importance of the sisterhood in the life of his beautiful family.

Never underestimate the power of sisterhood – when a woman is loved and nurtured by all, she is happy and content. Have courage to call on old friends and make new ones. Add each pearl of the sisterhood to *your* tapestry of life.

Birth is the New Beginning

Claire looked out of her window at the clear night sky. It was a crisp night with a hint of snow in the air. She stood in the darkness with her arms wrapped tightly around her. A shiver ran down her spine. Not a cold shiver; more a feeling of apprehension that filled her being. 'What if I can't handle this new beginning?' she quietly asked herself.

Claire had always been good at being a confidante to others. She offered sound advice, encouraging them to take brave steps on life's journey. However, when it came to taking her own advice, Claire quivered in her boots. She lacked the most important ingredient of all when it came to taking a chance on life; self confidence.

Claire reached down and placed a hand on her abdomen. She did this instinctively, not really knowing why.

'I know how much I want this,' she thought, 'but am I ready?' How many times had she asked that same question of herself throughout her life?

The twinkling stars in the indigo sky grabbed Claire's attention as they seemed to grow brighter, but she shrugged off the thought as her over-active imagination.

'Who am I kidding,' she whispered. 'I am not capable; not good enough. I don't have the support I need.' Her narrow shoulders slumped as she continued to look out her window. What was she waiting for: a sign that declared that she was ready; she was worthy? Did she want a neon billboard in the night sky that read, 'Claire, go for it!'? She giggled at the thought of her very own night-time neon sign.

Her lip curled as she felt the old pangs of anxiety reach into the depths of her being. All she had ever wanted was to have something of her very own. Something she had personally created.

Claire felt that she had been preparing her whole life to give birth and yet she still doubted that her preparations were enough. Would they ever be enough in her critical eyes?

The stars twinkled brightly once more and Claire caught a glimmer of movement; then another and another. Flashes of intense light bombarded the night sky. The timing of this superb light show was not lost on her.

She stood in awe of the magnificence of the meteor shower she was witnessing. Claire immediately understood the significance of the messages and the signs she was receiving throughout this timely event. This was indeed her own neon billboard, and it was saying loud and clear, 'Claire, go for it!'

Instinctively, both of her hands were now resting gently on her belly. She felt a warmth emanating from deep within her. Her inner fire was ignited. It had been lit long ago when she had first dreamt about an idea for helping humanity, a strategy for global change, and peace for people everywhere.

She dreamt it; played with it and often shelved it with excuses of 'not the right time; I'm too busy; I will be ridiculed; it won't work. Who am I to think I could dream up a solution to certain global issues?'

Claire had written and expanded her dream until this moment when doubt had again threatened to smother her with insatiable and numbing fear.

Then a glorious shower of light had signalled a new birth; the birth of her long-held dream. Light would always shine the way; she would always be supported. Claire knew she would never be alone.

You see, in that shower of light, a reflection glowed in the window of her world. A reflection that showed a young woman and man; *this* woman and her young husband staring out of this same window – so long ago.

He, with his arms around her; hands on her pregnant belly; due to give birth any day. On that night, as they looked out at the night sky, a meteor shower had gifted them with a light show they had never before seen.

Claire was so much older now; her beautiful child grown; her husband had died long ago. And yet, in those few moments; standing at that window, witnessing the light, she felt his warm arms around her, his hands on her belly. She could hear his whispered words, that miracles happen and it was time to birth her dream. He would always be with her.

Humanity needed her to live her dream; finally.

It was no longer the fearful apprehension she felt deep within her. Anticipation and excitement had replaced it. There was a big world outside that window and Claire had just glimpsed some of its awesome magic.

The Painting

The girl stopped to listen.

Someone was following her.

She slowly turned around. There was no-one to be seen.

She continued on her way.

There it was again.

The rustle of silk.

Now she could also smell a faint fragrance.

Floral.

It made her think of something.

What was it?

Gone now.

There it was again.

The rustle of silk. The faint floral fragrance.

But now there was something else.

A warmth she could feel but could not determine its whereabouts.

Gone again.

Can't quite grasp why these were all so familiar.

No fear.

Puzzled though.

Why was she here?

She had never been here and yet she knew this place well.

She knew exactly where she was going.

Up and up two flights of stairs. How did she know there were two?

The old brass doorknob opened beneath her fingers. She knew what
she would find beyond the heavy wooden door.

Directly opposite her was a woman.

It was like looking directly into her own eyes.

It was her own mouth; her own nose.

A beautiful old painting of days long gone.

But the memories – faint – remain untouched by time.

The rustle of silk comes closer, the floral fragrance stronger, the warmth all-encompassing as though arms are gently embracing her – reaching out from another time and place.

As the feelings begin to fade her mother speaks softly, 'this is your Great-Great Grandmother child'.

The child smiles and reaches out a hand to gently trace the contours of the face in the painting.

Acceptance comes.

Recognition awakens.

She is the reincarnation of her very own Great-Great Grandmother.

She smiles a knowing smile and vows to continue the work she began more than a century ago.

At only four years old, she knows her true destiny lies within the walls of this room.

She is a seer.

She will now be accepted for what she is.

This time she will not die of ridicule and persecution.

What was left undone; will now be complete.

Patience and Dreams

Every day the local children gathered together in the forest. They ran, played, swam in the creek, rested, ate their sandwiches and generally had a good time. They played hide and seek amongst the ancient trees and climbed high into the branches.

In the centre of this playground of trees grew a beautiful white-trunked tree – a ghost gum. Strangely, the children never went near the tree; never touched its trunk or sat with their backs against it as they ate their lunches.

The tree desperately wanted to be a part of their games; he longed for the touch of their innocent hands upon his trunk. This tree was a young tree compared to the ancient tall trees around him. He didn't even look like the other trees; with their dark bark and low-hanging branches.

When he asked the wise old trees why he wasn't included in the children's games, they laughed and said he was too small and insignificant. They said 'look at you, all white and straight. We, on the other hand, have branches to be climbed and our roots run above the ground, as well as below; a great place to sit and rest. Your roots just go into the earth.

The tree had his answers and yet he still yearned for the children to notice him; to play with him.

He thought long and hard about how he could achieve his dream. No amount of thinking would yield him an answer. As time went by and the children grew bigger; they didn't often come into the forest; too busy with other things in their life to play anymore.

The tree eventually decided it was time to stop worrying about his need for the laughter and touch of the children. He let go of his dream.

Time passed, and he continued to grow tall and straight until his branches reached higher than the rest of the canopy of the forest. He could see the whole world from up here. Not only that; but more and more animals made their homes in the hollows of his trunk; birds made their nests in his branches. He was content in knowing that he was refuge to many.

One day, an elderly woman came venturing into the forest. As she walked, she touched some of the trees; her face a picture of remembering times long past. She could almost hear the laughter of her childhood as she and her friends hid amongst the trees.

The white-trunked tree became aware of this elderly woman. He instantly recognised her as one of the local children who had played in the forest. Was it really so long ago?

Along with that memory came the old feelings; the yearning to be touched by children.

The tree was now so tall and graceful that he stood out from the other trees. He glowed in his uniqueness. He had grown into the wise ways of the world.

The elderly woman stopped and with a sharp intake of breath she said out loud, 'I remember you. I always noticed you, but the other children wanted to play in the branches and the roots of the bigger trees. I am so happy to see how tall you have become. I was afraid you would be destroyed if we played on you when you were still only a young tree.'

The woman reached forward to place her hands and forehead on the massive trunk of the tree. She then turned and sat with her back leaning against it. She sighed and the tree felt his dream had just been realised.

The woman began to speak. 'I had to come back to the place of innocence I knew as a child. My grown-up life has not been easy and now I am dying. My heart is failing. I had to come back you see; I wanted to hear the laughter; I wanted to feel the joy of being amongst the trees. I wanted to see how *your* life had fared; if you had survived and thrived. I can see that you have, and it makes my journey easier now.'

The woman was silent and in her silence; in that place of innocence, she felt something – an embrace; a loving embrace that gave her courage and strength to take on the next stage of her journey. The woman relaxed into the embrace; knowing that it came from the tree. In that moment they were one; each sharing something special with the other. No need for words; the inner knowing was enough.

The woman finally got up and turned to face the tree. 'As my time approaches to leave this world, I will now do so with courage and strength. I will remember you – always.'

It had taken many years for the tree to accomplish his dream and he was glad that time had come full circle and that he had finally felt the hands of a child upon his trunk. He knew now that his dream had a greater purpose; he was supposed to wait, to surrender the dream in order to be all that he was supposed to be, and in the end; in those few precious moments, his dream came true.

He had grown into his wisdom so that he could share that wisdom with the child who was now a woman and ready to make the ultimate transition. He had lived his life so far, just for this moment. He felt very blessed.

Dreams do come true. The tree had learned the importance of surrender and patience and living life, because *they* are the keys to so much learning and experience about our life journey.

Simplicity and Gratitude

The woman flung her arms in the air in exasperation. 'I can't do this anymore!' she exclaimed. 'There is never enough money to do the things I want to do. I always seem to come last in this household. You are a bunch of selfish hypocrites. You say you love me and then you always hold out your hands for money. I need money for school, for the movies; the latest gadget; the latest clothes, you say. I always give each of you everything you ask for. Well, I've had it. I quit!'

The woman retreated to her bedroom to sulk. 'I'll show them a thing or two,' she thought. 'I'll just stay here a while, and they can get their own meals.'

She was feeling very unappreciated, as usual. She gave them everything, and she received nothing in return. The woman sat there wallowing in her anger; trying to think of ways to get back at them. 'Selfish they are – all of them.'

Finally, the woman's anger began to lessen and, in her solitude, she began to think of ways she could get them to love her; to appreciate what she did for them every day. She already gave them every material thing they desired. They were all nearly grown now and still they treated her like a slave.

The anger returned, and she ranted at herself for being weak; for needing her family's approval. The woman paced the floor, despairing that anything would ever change in her household. She thought of withholding privileges to get them to notice the things she did for them.

She thought of running away from home for a few days, but that wouldn't work either; the housework would still be there for her when she returned. Instead, the woman decided to do something for herself. She picked up her handbag and car keys and promptly left the house, stating that she wouldn't return until much later in the day.

Her children just raised their eyebrows at each other as though to say, 'here she goes again; throwing a tantrum.' They let her go; best not to mess with her when she was in 'one of her moods'.

This attitude exasperated the woman even more. Did no-one understand and appreciate her? She aimlessly drove around awhile – not knowing where she really wanted to go.

The woman got lost, not realising how far she had driven. She was in a town she had never visited. She drove slowly into the town centre, past dilapidated buildings and shop fronts with boarded-up windows. The woman stopped her car and got out, with no idea where she was. Just then, she saw a group of children playing in the street. The children had made a circle in the dirt and a couple of the older children had some marbles. The colourful spheres mesmerised the younger ones.

The children looked up as the woman approached them. They were dirty and unkempt and yet all the faces that looked up at her had big beaming smiles. They were happy to see someone new in town.

Other than these few children, there was no-one else around. 'Where is everyone?' she asked them.

'There is no-one else,' they replied, 'we are alone. We have each other.'

'Where are the adults; your parents?' the woman asked.

'Dead,' an older boy said without emotion.

'How?' she wondered aloud.

'The war,' another boy replied.

The woman thought she must be going mad. 'Where are we?' she asked.

'Sierra Leone,' they replied as they continued playing their game.

'I can't be in Sierra Leone – I am in Australia'.

'Where is Australia?' They kept playing their simple game as though it was the most important thing in the world. They laughed together when the marbles clinked as they played.

The woman sat down heavily in the dirt near them. She didn't know what to make of all this. How could she be driving around her local townships in Australia one minute and then be somewhere else; some other country, the next?

She placed her head on her knees and hugged her arms around her. She didn't know how long she stayed like that, but she became aware of the night sky descending around her. She raised her head and gasped in shock as the scene around her was not the town she had driven to in the afternoon; but she was now in her own bedroom. She was sitting on the floor under her bedroom window.

I must have fallen asleep – a dream, she thought. What an amazing dream it was. So full of personal insights about how selfish *I* am and how I can *still* teach my children the art of simple gratitude.

She knew what she had to do. The world she and her family lived in was one of material gain in exchange for gratitude. After her dream 'visit' to Sierra Leone, the woman understood that it is the simplicity of life for which we need to be grateful.

She would go and hug her children and tell them how much they are loved and appreciated. She would show them by example not through financial incentives, what it is like to hold gratitude for life and its wealth of experiences.

The woman stood, ready to enter the chaotic world of her adored family. A family she would not give up if her life depended on it. She brushed down her skirt and a little pile of dirt fell around her feet; just like the dirt on which she had sat in her 'dream' state. Had she really 'visited' Sierra Leone whilst still in her bedroom? She didn't know how that was possible. What she did know was that the dirt around her would serve as a tangible reminder of the gratitude one must hold for the simplicity and sacredness of life; especially gratitude for the loving arms of her glorious family.

Life can be extinguished at any time through any circumstance. The woman understood just how blessed she was to live her life surrounded by an abundance of noisy teenagers. *Her* job as their parent was to teach them by being a living example of loving them without expectation and sometimes, with tough love. They may not 'get it' at first, but she is tough, and in time they will come to understand that it is the simple things in life that warrant *real* gratitude and appreciation.

Journey of the Heart

Faith! That unfathomable, undeniable expression of truth.

Faith! In what? In ourselves? In each other? In our political systems? In religion? In the processes of life?

So where is mine? Did I ever have it? Will I ever feel it? Where does one feel faith?

Mary says she has faith in me. She is my best friend. She's prejudiced. *I* don't have faith in myself.

Why does my decision have to be based on faith? Why can't it be made by weighing up the pros and cons? Isn't that how it's meant to be done?

Surely, she jests. Believe in myself, she says. Have a little faith. *She* doesn't have to make this decision.

My mind is full of what ifs, buts and maybes.

Ask your heart, she says. Do I have a heart?

It has been broken so many times. I'm not sure it exists anymore.

She scoffs at me. Everyone has a heart. Try to think with your heart, she says.

How, I ask? Logic will surely see me through. No emotion in logic. My heart brought to bear too much unwanted emotion.

Cold, she says. I'm not cold! Am I? Well, am I?

I've had to protect myself. Failure hurts.

She tells me there is no decision to make. It's too late for decisions.

The pain comes again and I realise that it really is too late for decisions. I will just have to take the consequences – whatever they may be.

One final long pain and I am handed a tiny bundle. My eyes are closed. I can't look.

Mary whispers, 'she's perfect'.

I open my eyes and gaze in wonder at the wisdom and love in the eyes staring back at me.

What is that I feel?

'Your heart,' says Mary.

Dance

Dance in the moonlight
Swim in the stream
Walk in the sunshine
Dream wondrous dreams

Life is for living
The best that we can
But sometimes we must face
The shadows of our clan

It's not always perfect
As we walk through this life
But love walks within us
Helping us challenge the strife

So, dance in that moonlight
And swim in that stream
When you walk in the sunshine
You will live that dream

When the moment is harsh
And it's hard to draw breath
Think of the sunshine
And breathe in your strength

It's *born* of the sunshine,
The moon and the stars
This strength that we bear
Will heal our wounds and scars

Dance in the moonlight
Sing in the rain
Don't waste a moment
When there's so much to gain

Love is for all
It doesn't compete
Love is a joy
That helps us find our feet

Dance in the moonlight
Dance with delight
There's a new chapter waiting
In the wings for us to write

Dreams

Dream the big dreams
And the little ones too
Dream the everyday dreams
And high-flying dreams anew

Some dreams arrive
The moment you express them in your heart
Many take a lifetime
Just remember it's the start

Dreams grow and change
With every twist and turn
Shining a light on the way
Once begun there's no return

Taking journeys to unknown places
Until your dream becomes clear
With an inner knowing that your dream path
At any moment could appear

Dreams are just one way
Of showing us our worth
One of many tools
That keep us stepping upon this earth

Dreams are always worthy
None too big or too small
As we clear away life's debris
We create for one and all

You see dreams are for everyone
As we step toward unity
When we share in our creations
We awaken an amazing opportunity

So, dream in the life
You want to see created
With heart driven purpose
It's been so long awaited

Dreams create freedom
Of the spirit within
A belief in something more
That's our place to begin

Caught in a world of chaos
Can dampen the shiniest dreams
But that dream is never lost
It can always be redeemed

Dreams live in your heart
Just a spark of light away
Ignite them once more
It's a brand-new bright day

The Simple Life

There's no time to waste
Said all the busy people.
Robots of life
Each taking turns
At being the hare
In the story of old.
Stress marks the spot
Where the faster one travels
Success is assured, right?
Failure is marked with denial
Of its important
Learning potential
In this chaotic
Consumer driven world.
Simple life.
What a joke
Said all the busy people.
Earn more,
Play less.
Bigger
Better
Debt.
Advertising sucks at your earnings
Like a gambling addiction
Of must haves.
Busyness creates poverty
Of a different kind
Beholden to the corporations

That speak
Words of false promises
Wearing charming masks
Telling all comers
I have the answer
To your wants
Your needs.
This busy world
Must change.
Invite simplicity in.
Do not mistake simple life
With being poor
Second best.
The simple life…
Creates more
Not less.

How do I Really Want to live?

How do I really want to live?
Is this a question we have asked ourselves?
Or is this the question we have avoided
Caught in a world of consumerism
Debt
Fear
Must do
Must have
Be someone
Something
Go here
There
Anywhere but where I am.
Busy
Busy
Busy
Caught in a trap of our own making.
Perhaps the question should be
How can I change it
To live the life I want to live
Be the person I want to be
In simplicity
At peace with my geography
My world around me.
Loved
Loving
Conscious living
Setting my own pace

Taking time out to breathe
To see a new view
To hear the sounds of nature
Renewed
Answerable to myself
Walking in balance
On a pathway of my choosing.
When that pathway
Is littered with chaos
Division
I will find my own way
Back to me.
The revolution of self
Will bring understanding
And ultimately togetherness
When we appreciate
Who we are first
In a world
Where everyone
Is minding everyone else's business.

Live a Little... Live a Lot

When something seems different to all the rest
Embrace it
Explore it
Try it on for size
See if it fits with where you are going
Does it touch your heart?
Does it move you into joy?
Who wants to be like all the rest?
Who wants to do more of the same?
Think outside the box life put you in; a proverbial square peg in a
    round hole
Live a little
Live a lot
Be unique
Be yourself
You don't have to be a shadow of someone else's journey
We are curious creatures, but habitual busyness for busy sake can hide
    precious experiences in plain sight
Things we might not notice until others are seeing beauty in something
    as simple as springtime blossom
A falling leaf
The turn of a season
The birth of a new day full of promise for life beyond the mundane
    and busy
There is music to be heard in the winds in the treetops
In the birdsong
In the rolling thunder
And the mighty crack of lightning

In the way the ocean tides ebb and flow

There's a box waiting for each of us at the end of life

But in the meantime

Don't let anyone

I mean *anyone*... put you in a box and label you the same as anyone else

Live a little

Live a lot

See what's all around you

Break old habits

Dance in the rain

Turn your face toward the sunshine

Feel the sand between your toes

Explore the wilderness

Explore your own wildness

Be passionate about life

Be love

Be outrageous when the mood takes you

Laugh until you snort... gasp for air and your belly hurts from a simple pleasurable moment of pure silliness

It stretches time when you open the chapter marked 'you are here'...

Explore a world beyond... well... here

A few steps to the north, the south, the east or the west will lead you into a new adventure

A few moments watching the stars, a sunrise, a leaf twirling to the ground can open you to something profound, amazing, fabulous, awesome

In that opening lies the secrets of your own unique universe!

A moment can seem like an hour

An hour can seem like three

Time becomes irrelevant in those moments

A gift from your soul

A crack in time to see a new view

A time to be inspired to create something meaningful

In your work, your relationship, your health

Think and feel outside the ordinary

Think and feel through the filter of heart centred joy
Nature is designed to inspire
She is just waiting for your input
In those shared spaces
She opens her classroom to you
So that you may learn more
About your own… universe… within

What If?

What if
You not only craved freedom of the spirit within
But lived it in every way possible
What if
You danced to the beat of your own drum
And taught others how to dance
What if
You spoke from your heart
Every day, every moment, every opportunity you had to speak with love
What if
You healed your wounds of the past
And lived for today
What if
You made new plans, broke invisible rules
And lived your life your way
What if
When you walked in nature
You felt alive, vibrant, reborn, renewed
What if
You opened a door of opportunity
And changed the status quo
What if
You found your voice, your courage
To transform something from old to gold on your journey
What if
Life stopped being 'what if'
And became your reality
What if

You took a chance on you
And lived life on your terms
What if
This is a year for transformation
For you and those you love
What if
Can become a regret
If you don't take a chance on you
Make the 'what if's' in your life your natural way of living
They're not an add-on to your life
They are as natural as breathing
Make a choice
Hold no regrets
Be who you want to see in your world
Life's a perfectly imperfect journey but it's a heck of a ride!

Will I?

You turn your face to the sky
Raindrops fall
Gentle rhythmic splashes
Washing clean old pains and suffering
No longer needed
As you walk a new path through life.
A breeze caresses you
Warm
Cool
Wrapping you in a cloak of deep mystery
The unknown becoming known
Only when the next step is ready to be taken.
Turn slowly in all directions
East, north, west and south
Returning to the east
Feeling the wholeness of the circle of life.
Drink in the beauty around you
With eyes that see beyond the ordinary world
To the extraordinary
To the magic that exists beyond everyday thought.
It's likely more than you know
As it touches your heart
Awakens your soul journey
Your destiny.
In the quiet of your heart
This magic creates an opportunity
To open your mind to new possibilities.
Can I?

Should I?
Will I?
You will ask.
An open heart
An inquiring mind
Witnessed in the beauty of your surroundings
Will show you the steps to walk
If only
You are willing
To take a chance on you.

Unfurling of the Feminine Spirit

Feminine spirit
Sacred
Sensual
Warm and loving

She is awakening
Unfurling
Stretching
Pivoting

This oft elusive woman is hiding in plain sight; her curves deemed a
flaw in an outdated world
Her breasts too small, too big, overly sexual
Her body a temple and a temptation.

This woman is becoming liberated from patriarchal musings about who
she should be.
She is a butterfly emerging languorously from her cocoon; a
magnificent resilient aroused fluid woman... gloriously transformed
by her own inner workings.

She moves sensuously to the beat of her own drum.
She stirs the senses in all she encounters on her travels through life.

Feminine spirit
Powerful
Wild
Wilful
Ready to walk a path not yet travelled in this changing world.

The awakened sacred, sensual feminine spirit guides her pack out of the fiery chaos rampaging our world and into a spirited, passionate encounter with her own feminine spirit.

I bow to your feminine spirit...

Life is a Mystery

Open a door to the mysteries of the Universe
Open it to the mysteries of your own world
To the mysteries of your own geography.
Above all
Open that door to the mysteries of your heart and soul.
We all have access to the mysteries of life
We just need to be willing to look… see and experience.
We just need to explore beyond the everyday
To push beyond the limitations and boundaries we are told exist.

Soul Song

I sit by the flickering flames as they dance and crackle
Warmth settles lightly on my skin, but not enough to burn
A gentle golden glow nurtures my weary heart
My breath is deep… slow and steady
My heartbeat sounds like a drumbeat in my ears… beating a rhythmic
    cadence that matches the tune played by the dancing sacred fire
A billion stars shine their light overhead in the inky dark sky
No moon
No breeze
No worries in these precious moments
I begin to sway to music only I can hear
My soul song; beautiful… meditative
My feet move with a flow that I seem to instinctively know
A sequence of sacred steps repeated over and over in time to my song
Faster and faster, I dance
Until
The music within me stops
The quiet is absolute
Everything around me is frozen in time
A gap between thoughts
Between heartbeats
I am a woman
Caught between realities
A precious gift in the crack formed between places
A single thought settles willingly into my heart
I am love… I love and I am loved
Nothing else exists *except* love
That is the reality of our Universe

I bow in acknowledgement of this message
And return to the song of love from my soul
The crackling fire
And the starry heavens
But all is different
All is changed
I am different
I am changed
And that's all about love

Sacred Woman

Sacred Woman of now
Step into your light
As we move through the darkness
We will open to sacred sight

Eyes shining bright
Embracing feminine power
Halting patriarchal struggles
This…. is the feminine hour

Stand up and shout
Let the world hear our cry
Into battle we gallop
Swords of wisdom held high

No time to waste
The battle lines are drawn
The feminine is moving
Old powers are being withdrawn

Sacred Woman of light
There is no denying
We've been told a lie
That we're no longer buying

The truth of the matter
Is the feminine is revising
A steep curve of learning
For the new powers uprising

Stand and be counted
Feet firmly upon the earth
The sanctity of all life
Begins with our rebirth

Sacred Woman of power
Grandmother wisdom keeper
Blessed days of remembering
We will no longer be considered weaker

Sacred womb of the earth
Keeper of birth, life and death
Masters of mystery
Until we take our last breath

Sacred woman of light
It's now we are needed
Standing shoulder to shoulder
Woman's power won't be depleted

Archaic; once called power
Is now under review
Old ways no longer relevant
Feminine spirit stands tall and true...

Healing Prayer — say prior to any healing work

I call on the spirits; the Council of Healers
Bring forward this healing
As we journey through love
Whatever is needed
Is sealed from above
Fire & air
Water and earth
The spirit within
Embraces new birth
Healing the spirit
The body and mind
We seek a new pathway
Now the three are aligned
Seal in the light
Let the past be gone
The present is healed
The heart is now strong…

Journey

I journey alone
I journey as one
And yet I am never alone
For I am one of many.
When the many are divided
We create anarchy and dissension.
When the many are one
Our journey is tempered with love.
I am proud to be one of many
And I am proud that many are one.

The Mirror

The mirror we look into everyday
Reflects truth in our lives.
We cannot hide behind the façade
We build up around ourselves any longer.
Look hard and deep
And you may be pleasantly surprised
By what you see.

Peace

Peace is being at one with self
Peace is the joy of being with a loved one
Peace is the serenity which comes from within
Peace is sitting by a gently flowing river
Peace is the blue of the morning sky
Peace is the accomplishment of a smile complete
Peace is sharing yourself with others
Peace is remarkable when it touches your soul.

It's Never Too Late

His mind was racing, as it always did upon waking. His earliest memory was of a mind filled with hopes, dreams, ideas and enthusiasm. As he grew, his thoughts changed. Now his mind was filled with fear, anger and blame. How and when did he change?

He actually knew the answer to this. He could pinpoint the exact moment in his life when nothing was ever the same again. He had been having wonderful thoughts as usual and on this particular day he decided he would like to share them. Who better to share his dreams with than his mother. Mothers were encouraging and understood, didn't they?

He found his mother at the kitchen sink preparing the evening meal.

'Mum' he said, 'I've got something on my mind that I would really like to share with you.'

She looked at him closely and saw happiness spread across his face.

He told her his 'angel' had visited him and told him something wonderful.

Before he could tell her more, she turned and told him that was a lot of fanciful rubbish. There were no such things as angels. They were only in people's imaginations. She told him he was 'too old' for imaginary friends and that he should bring his mind into the real world and stop dreaming. She told him she was busy and to go away and leave her alone.

The person he trusted most had just shattered everything he believed to be true.

He thought there was something wrong with him. He never again shared any of his thoughts with anyone. He was fearful of rejection and ridicule. He became introverted and lost. He drifted through life in fear.

Today was his 50th birthday. Just another day, really. He supposed he should visit his mother. She was quite elderly and ill now, and looked forward to his visits.

He sat up and shook his head as though trying to clear his mind. Today there was a new thought in his head. He tried to grasp it, but it seemed just out of reach. Never mind, he'd leave it and go and have a shower.

There was that thought again – a little stronger now. He recognised the thought but didn't know where from. Aaaah, his early childhood came flooding back and with it came his hopes and dreams. With it came the image of his 'angel'. He thought he had long suppressed these imaginings, but then something happened to help him know his angel was real.

A feeling he hadn't experienced since childhood enveloped him. It started in his heart and spread to cover him like a warm embrace. The room glowed brighter and a faint image appeared before him as it once had in childhood. 'Do you remember when you were going to share a wonderful thought with your mother?' the angel whispered. 'It is never too late for sharing ourselves and our hopes and dreams with others.'

He visited his mother that day with renewed hope in his heart that she would indeed accept him this time. They sat together at the kitchen table to share a moment on his birthday. His mouth was dry as he prepared to speak. Before he could say what was on his mind, his mother said, 'I was visited by an angel today and he told me something wonderful'.

The Healer

The healer went to the well. There she met a man in a long, white robe. As she approached the well, he spoke to her softly and said, 'I was to sent to help you.'

The healer asked the man, 'in what way can you help me?'

'I was sent to give you the gift of enlightenment, but first, you must complete three tasks.'

The healer had never seen anybody like this man, and yet he seemed familiar. He appeared ageless and his blue piercing eyes seemed to bore straight into her soul, as though he knew everything there was to know about her.

Instead of fear, she felt as though she was in the presence of an old friend. His manner was warm and loving. He appeared to glow from his very being. Although the healer had just met him, she had total trust in what he was about to ask of her.

The man said, 'when you return to your home, you are to go within for seven days and seven nights and think of nothing. This is your first task.'

'When you have accomplished this, your second task is to go into nature and listen to the birds, to the trees and to the wind and the streams.'

'When you have completed both of these tasks successfully, I will return to inform you of your third and last task.'

The healer took a deep breath and turned to return home. She prepared herself for her first task. She went into her sanctuary to light a candle and create an ambient setting for this task.

'This should not be too hard,' she thought. 'I'm a healer. I'm aware of the spiritual nature of all things.'

As the healer lay down and prepared to go within, she suddenly remembered people she had promised to see. The healer thought to herself, 'well, it doesn't have to begin right now; I'll begin after I've seen my friends'.

When she returned, she lay down in her special place and closed her eyes. There was a knock at the door. She went to answer it and again rejected the need to go within. Each time she attempted to go within and think no thoughts, something would announce its arrival in her head or her environment and deter her from the task the man at the well had set for her.

'I can't do this,' she thought. 'I believed I was spiritual enough to do anything that was asked of me. I can't even pass the first task.' Having recognised the problem of putting everything else first instead of the needs of herself, the healer was well on the way to completing her first task.

Next, she ventured into nature, thinking what an easy task this would be. She had been into nature many times. She'd heard the sounds of the birds, the rustling leaves of the trees as they swayed in the breeze, the trickling of the streams as they meandered over smooth rocks and the whistling of the wind on a stormy day. Task number two was a cinch!

As the healer wandered deeper into the bush, she became aware of a silence she had never before experienced. As she listened to the silence, she slowly became aware of other sounds.

Instead of the normal sounds a bird makes, or a tree or stream, or the wind, she heard words and songs. There were messages coming from all around her.

So, this is what the man in the white robe wanted her to experience. It was beyond her imagination; beyond her limited view of the spiritual nature of *all* life. What a wonderful task he had set for her.

The healer returned to the well, where she again met the man. He was already aware of how she had fared in her first two tasks. The answer to both shone from her heart, her eyes, and her whole being. Her face glowed with the sheer joy of experience.

'Task number three,' he told her, 'is to take the knowledge you have learned from your first two tasks and apply them to your healing work.' He announced he would return in one year's time.

With renewed confidence, the healer began incorporating her new-found knowledge into healing. However not everyone wanted to know about these things.

She became disheartened. How was she going to complete task number three when people wouldn't accept what she was trying to do?

Suddenly a thought occurred to her. Why not go within to find the answer; why not visit nature and ask the birds, the trees, the streams and the wind!

The healer did these things and was told the following message.

Heal with your heart
And let others accept love
If they want to experience
The joys your knowledge can bring.

If unable to accept
Feel safe and secure
Knowing you have done all you can
To bring joy to their hearts and souls.

Renewed with hope, the healer continued to work in this way. One year later, the healer again went to the well and met the man in the long white robe. He told her she had travelled far along the path of enlightenment. She had already received the gift of enlightenment by opening herself up to receive the messages of spirit.

If we do not seek reward, we shall be rewarded when we least expect it. Our higher self is always waiting to help us. It doesn't matter if it is by a well or within our own heart; our soul is ready to enlighten us.

Magic

Magic is in the air. I can feel it as though it is a physical thing. I woke this morning to a perfect blue-sky day. The birds were singing and my heart was full of joy. I bounced eagerly out of bed so that I didn't waste a moment of it. Something special was going to happen today. I don't know how I knew this, I just knew. I looked in the mirror, and for no particular reason there was a huge smile on my face. I positively glowed with happiness.

Showered, dressed and ready for anything, I decided to go for a long walk in the glorious sunshine. The green of the trees seemed brighter, their branches bending toward me in greeting. The colours of the flowers in the gardens I passed seemed to touch my very soul. The people I met greeted me like long-lost friends, even though I had never seen them before.

I entered a nearby park and sat on the soft grass. I drank in every detail around me. Nothing escaped my notice. It was as though every one of my senses was heightened on this most perfect of days.

A huge golden dog bounced my way, tail wagging. He licked my face and bounded off in another direction, answering the call of his master. I don't know how long I spent sitting in that park, but I decided to be on the move again. A cartwheel or two; a hop, skip, and a jump. I hadn't felt so alive in years.

I started to tire. I had walked a long way and still had to make my way home. I turned back. The closer to home I got – the faster my pace became. It was as though an invisible cord was pulling me home.

Soon I was standing on my very own threshold. There were questions in my mind. I wanted to remain free in the sunshine, but something kept pulling at me. I edged my way inside, not wanting to give up my freedom yet. I couldn't hold on to this beautiful feeling any longer. I had to go back inside, back home.

What are all these tubes in my arms? What is attached to my head and chest?

Why are my loved ones standing over me? I'm frightened – I want to walk again in the sunshine. I want to be free.

'You're back,' they say.

'From where?' I ask.

'Son, you've been in a coma for five days and half an hour ago we nearly lost you, but you came back to us.'

'We love you son'.

The Lavender Lady

I peered over the fence to another time, a seemingly different world where a cottage garden bloomed on this warm summer's morning. So many flowers. So many fragrances. I had walked by this place many times, but I had never stopped to take it all in. Closing my eyes for a moment, I breathed deeply of the many fragrances but one in particular tantalised my senses. I knew it from my childhood. It was the smell of lavender, and it reminded of my grandmother, the beautiful anchor in my life that I had just lost to illness.

Given what I was going through in this moment, I remembered times with her baking in her kitchen, and playing in her garden. They are among my favourite memories. The tears threatened to fall. My thoughts were to quickly move along before I made a fool of myself right there in the street.

Just as I was about to turn back to the footpath, a clear, slightly accented, sing song voice called out. 'Would you like to come in and have tea with me?' I looked around for the source of the voice. I spotted an elderly lady sitting on a white wicker chair on the veranda of the house. She smiled at me and I was lost to my grief. I opened the gate and walked up the path toward her. I didn't know her, but I did too. She was so like the beautiful woman I had just lost.

As I approached she said, 'take a seat and I'll go and put the kettle on.' She hadn't asked me who I was, or anything at all. She simply made me feel at home with those simple words. She was so like my grandmother. Welcoming, beautiful and kind-hearted.

The elderly woman stood and brushed down her full apron. Her sensible shoes and stockings just peeking out below a long flowing dress that seemed timeless in its simplicity. Her silver hair was piled up messily on top of her head, giving her a rather beautiful and stylish look.

Actually, her narrow face was so alive and animated rather than beautiful. Her bright blue eyes sparkled with mischief and joy. Here was a woman, I thought, who epitomised the grandmother look and combined it with simple elegance.

'I'll be right back', she said. 'Oh, and you can just call me Nanna.'

I sat on the other wicker chair on Nanna's veranda and surveyed her fabulous garden from a different angle. It was even more wonderful from this side of the fence. I sat back and closed my eyes again. This time, as I breathed in the fragrances of the garden, I allowed the tears to flow.

I'm not sure how much time passed, but it only felt like seconds. My hostess was again seated beside me and a tea tray with a large old-fashioned teapot and two beautiful teacups were placed on the table between us. A plate of homemade teacake was also on the wicker table. I say table loosely, but really it was like a scene from a bygone era. There was an intricately needle-pointed tea cloth and pretty serviettes, along with matching plates. How on earth had she set this all up without me noticing!

Nanna must have guessed my thoughts because she smiled and said, 'I'm a master of tea ceremony and, after all my years on this planet, I know how to quietly set a table.'

My tears threatened again. Nanna gently laid her hand on mine and simply said, 'let them flow, to let them go.'

Some time later, once the tears had been shed, Nanna poured the still-steaming tea into our cups and cut generous slices of teacake and put them on the plates.

'Thank you,' I said, 'for your kindness. I'm a stranger, and your generosity has helped me unleash some of my grief.'

'Oh, but you're not a stranger. You walk past here most days, always in a hurry. No time to stop and smell the lavenders. Today was the day meant for stopping and simply sitting with an old lady over tea and cake.'

'Now, as the lavenders have invited you to my garden, let me tell you my lavender story and how she helps people in need.'

'Lavender plants have been around for thousands of years and in my world, they have been a part of life handed down through my ancestors. You see, lavender speaks to me as she has spoken to many in my family line.'

'When I was just a wee child, I would sit in my grandmother's garden and the plants would talk to me. Aaahhhh, I can see that you too had such a connection with your grandmother.'

'It was one particular type of plant, the lavender plant, that spoke to me the loudest and longest. Whenever I was near, she would sway in the breeze and her fragrance would fill the garden. I learned to sit quietly with her and we would share tales of wonder. Or rather, I would ask a million questions and she would patiently answer where she could. She always spoke to me through my heart. Oh, the memories are mighty fine of those special times. She is so graceful and charming. Her manner calms even the wildest nerves. Her special fragrance calms the busiest of minds and eases the harshest grieving times, allowing peace to enter our hearts.'

'The story I am about to tell you though, is about how protective she is. I was born in Europe and lived there as a child during the war. I often stayed with my grandmother as my parents were busy doing work to help people escape to different countries. There were always soldiers around in the streets, but they never bothered me while I was playing in my grandmother's garden. I didn't bother them, so they didn't bother me.'

'One day though, my grandmother came and found me in the garden and told me to hide and to stay still and be quiet. She had a unique sixth sense when something was about to happen, so I never questioned her wisdom. I just did as I was told and looked for a place to hide.'

'The lavender bushes began to sway. I could hear soldiers opening our squeaky front gate and begin to walk up the garden path. They sounded angry to my young ears.'

'The lavender bushes swayed harder even though there was no breeze. I knew in that moment that I didn't have long to discover a hiding place and I jumped into the centre of the nearest lavender bush. Her flower stalks went so still. Her stems seemed to grow taller, covering me completely.'

'I could hear grandmother on her porch talking with the soldiers. They were asking where I was. They wanted to take me away to punish my parents and grandmother for helping their enemies. My grandmother stood up to them, all five feet of her and told them I wasn't there.

They didn't believe her and looked everywhere for me but of course they didn't think to look in the lavender bushes. They were angry at my grandmother, but she wouldn't tell them I was hiding in the garden. They shot her where she stood. I gasped, but the lavenders covered my sound with the rustling of their foliage.'

'I was eventually rescued and sent to another country for the rest of the war, but I grieved my grandmother all of my life. I honour her sacrifice by helping others on their journey. When the lavenders call to someone walking past my little abode and garden, I invite them in for tea and cake and storytelling.'

'I share this story with you because you too are grieving your grandmother who was taken too soon by an illness that invaded her body. She fought it, but ultimately it took her life.'

'Grandmothers are wise women with stories aplenty to share. Grieve, dear girl, but know she loved you and protected you all the days of her life.'

'Lavender brought you here to grieve and let the tears flow. They brought you to my garden to bring peace into your heart and healing into your soul. This is why lavenders are special. Plant your own lavender to honour your grandmother.'

'Now, drink your tea and eat your cake. I hope you will visit me often. The lavenders will always send you an invite on the breezes to come to tea and hear my stories!'

That day was the first day of my healing journey. Long after Nanna had also passed, I began to honour both women by inviting people to tea and cake and storytelling amongst the lavenders I have growing in my garden. Grandmother and Nanna would love that. The story of life continues.

The Wheelbarrow

The old man walked his wheelbarrow down the dusty country road most days. There was never anything in his wheelbarrow, but he always seemed to be carrying a heavy load. Most of his neighbours never asked him why he walked his wheelbarrow every day. They just stood at the windows of their houses and shook their heads.

'Oh well,' they all said, 'at least he seems harmless.' And they all went about their days.

One day, a young couple moved into the street. The neighbours talked amongst themselves. 'What's a young couple doing way out here?' they wondered.

So, they stood by their windows and shook their heads. 'At least they seem harmless,' they said. And they all went about their days.

They never noticed the despondency of the old man. They never noticed the sadness in the young woman's eyes or the helplessness in the young man's.

One sunny spring day, the young woman was working in her garden when she noticed the old man walk his wheelbarrow down the road. Curious, the young woman stood at her gate and said hello. The old man stopped and gave her a shy smile.

'G'day Mrs,' he said.

'Would you like to come in for a cuppa,' she asked?

The old man thought a moment before saying, 'that would be lovely'.

Now that gave the neighbours something to talk about. What could they be saying? What could they possibly have in common, the old man and the young woman?

'Oh well,' they all said as they stood at their windows, 'at least they seem harmless.' And they all went about their days.

The young woman asked the old man, 'why do you wheel your wheelbarrow down the dusty road every day?'

He thought a moment before whispering, 'I used to carry my wife in the wheelbarrow when she got too sick to walk. It was our fun outing where we still laughed like the youngsters we once were.'

'When we were courting, I used to pick her up and place her ever so gently in a wheelbarrow. I would push her like the queen she was. Anywhere she wanted to go.'

'When she got sick, I placed her gently in that wheelbarrow and again wheeled her wherever she wanted to go, even if it was in her imagination for a while. She was never a burden. I loved her so.'

'When she was gone, I was lost. So, on days like this, I carry her spirit in the old wheelbarrow, pretending she is the queen and I am at her service, taking her here and there.'

'Today,' the old man said gently, 'she would have loved having tea with a young lady with sad eyes.'

Quiet reigned for a few moments. The young woman began her story.

'A year ago, we lost our little boy. He was sick, you see. He was in a wheelchair and we would take him here and there. Wherever he wanted to be. Our little prince.'

'So, you see, we are not much different, you and me.'

The old man thought for a moment. He needed time to consider. 'How about we help each other? How about we use this old wheelbarrow to plant a new garden, start something new, you and me?'

The young woman placed her hand over the old man's. 'Yes,' she said, 'you and me.'

So, the young woman and the old man made a new garden. The young woman's husband was grateful to the old man. A smile had returned to his young wife's face. A smile that reached her eyes again. The old man felt he had purpose again. He called these young people family.

He smiled at his neighbours. They all came together to help each other now.

They no longer stood at their windows and wondered. They opened their doors and invited love in. It's as simple as that. When there is understanding after kindness, love flows. Always, in all ways.

The Angel

John was sitting with his elbows upon his knees, chin resting on the palms of his hands. What could he do today?

He could go and see the little blonde in the building at the corner of the street. Maybe he could go and visit his friend, Chris. There was always the little old lady who was always calling him. Or he could just hang out with the guys.

Decisions, decisions! Every time he visited one of his many friends, he ended up in trouble. Like the time the little blonde wanted the candles lit for a romantic dinner and he set the kitchen on fire. Or the time Chris' car wouldn't start and he flooded the engine. He knew he had to stop interfering in his friends' lives, but he just wanted to help people.

The only time he felt good about himself was when he visited the little old lady. She always seemed pleased to have him around. She liked to sit and talk to him for hours at a time.

Maybe he would just wander about and see what happened. Something happened alright. There he was, minding his own business, when out of nowhere came a woman who ran smack-bang straight into him. Odd, he thought. She didn't even seem to be aware of him. He became curious about why she was in such a hurry. He decided to follow her to see where she was going.

Keeping a safe distance, he quietly followed until he saw her stop and reach into her handbag for her keys. She fumbled for a moment in her obvious distress, then she opened the front lock and entered an old house.

She left the front door open in her hurry to get inside, so he decided to investigate. It was dark and cold and it took a moment to adjust his eyes to the low light.

At first, he couldn't find where the woman went. Then he heard her say quite clearly, 'Oh no Nan, please don't go. I'll miss you. What will I do without you?' The woman was crying softly.

He peered inside a beautiful room and saw a gentle elderly lady; *his* elderly lady lying in bed. She was dying. He could hear her voice, soft yet firm, say 'It's my time, child. Let me go. I am old and have lived a good life. The angels are here to make my journey easy.'

Calm settled in the room as it filled with brilliant light and the soft flutter of many wings. The old lady slipped quietly away and the woman felt suddenly alone. She kissed her Nan goodbye and whispered 'I love you, Nan.'

She slowly turned and saw him for the first time. Her eyes widened slightly and then she smiled, a sweet serene smile. The woman said 'thank you.'

John bowed his head in acknowledgement, spread his wings and slowly faded into the light.

Stormy Days of Grief

Clouds gallop across the sky
Black… ominous…
Heralding needed change.
Finally
Tears of release come
Pounding the earth with steady rhythmic plops.
Thunder roars
A wounded reverberation rages in the atmosphere.
Lightning cracks like a whip
Snapping power into the air.
Wind challenges the hardiest of souls
To withstand the might of the storm
Daring each to ignore the supernal power unleashed.
Feet planted on the earth
Woman lifts her face to greet the storm
Arching her back
Arms rising toward the darkened sky
Tears mingling with the heavy drops of rain.
Fists clenched
Rage palpable
She roars into the wind
Letting go her pent-up emotions
Stories stored
Waiting for this ultimate time of release.
Her fury spent
Sinking to the ground
Hands in the wet earth

Head bowed
The storm abates.
Stories washed clean
Grief pours from the open wounds of loss
Heart and soul healing has begun.

In the Eye of the Storm

In the eye of the storm
You will find your own peace
While the world rages violently
You will stand still and weep

Nothing to be done
Except hold the quiet space
Grief will flicker panic
When what is needed is grace

Weathering life's storms
Are lessons to learn
Challenges will be met
Doubt and fear the concern

In the eye of life's storms
Love will always arise
Clearing the debris
And dust from our eyes

Life can be turbulent
A pull on our heart
But in the eye of the storm
We move from chaos to hearth

When one stands in battle
To change tides of pain
Many will join them
There is so much to gain

Love will always thrive
And expand its holy hold
Grounded in its own power
Love can never be sold

It's worth more than money
But the corrupt one's greed
Seek only to bargain
With the devil's evil seed

Stand in the eye
Powerful in your peace
As love's sword ignites
The flame of change will increase

Wipe away your tears
Stand strong and hold your ground
The shaking earth will stop
Peace and love *will* finally be found

You Are Never Alone

When sadness walks with you
An angel is always by your side
You never have to walk alone

Your angel listens
As they gently rest their hand on your heart
A release to let the tears flow
No need to keep them in check

They hold you when times feel overwhelming
An angel hug wrapping you tight in their love

When you fall to your knees in despair
They kneel with you
Until you are ready to face the world again
They will help you to your feet
Hold you steady
And encourage you to take a deep healing breath

You see
We are never truly alone in our sadness
There is always someone there holding our hand
Keeping our heart safe when we don't have the strength to care

An angel is someone you can tell all to
They are never too busy
Never have something better to do
They will never judge
Nor will they measure your sadness with anyone else's

Angels exist in the non-physical and physical worlds...
They will always find you
You are never alone

Lonely in a Crowd

Lonely in a crowd
Isn't that the old cliché
And yet
The more we sit at our devices
The busier we are
The more we dissociate from nature
The more insular we make ourselves
The lonelier our world becomes.
Sigh
In our own stillness
In a crowded room
As the people race here
There
Everywhere
We are invisible
In this strange world
A stranger
In a strange land
Until…
We see another
And another
And another
Standing separate
In their own stillness.
Watching the busyness
Of the madding crowd
It becomes clear

They are alone
But not lonely
Never lonely
An oxymoron
A conflict of parts
Something unexplainable
But so perfect
In this crazy strange existence.
The one
Becomes many
And suddenly
They are no longer alone
And certainly never… ever…lonely

The Sacred Cauldron

Speak of the sacred cauldron
For change is now so near
Look into your reflection
A healer held so dear
The time and place are now
To stir the pot of life
When wisdom comes to visit
Release all painful strife
The healer deep within
Will show the mighty way
To keep the home fires burning
When there's nothing more to say
The time of change will come
When you sacrifice all that is lost
Remember the world begun now
Comes with only love's pure cost
It is only when you remember
The world is fresh and new
That the healer deep within you
Is always ready and true
Speak of the sacred cauldron
A tool for the ancient Crone
To journey to the realms of spirit
For reasons yet to be known
Her will is strong and courageous
As she chants over sacred bones
The time of the Crone is here now

Casting those ancient stones
There is always a sacred vow
When one speaks the truth of the heart
The sacred cauldron is waiting
For you to seek out its path

The Love on this Day

The love on this day
Is mine now to keep
The gateway has opened
To a new world born deep

A world I helped shape
With love from my heart
The gateway always open
A path to a new start

The first steps I take
Are love beyond exception
The Grace of the Mother
Re-birthed from conception

I choose now to see
A new way is dawning
Spreading my wings
I take flight; I am soaring

Heart Freedom

My Heart is open
It sets me free
To be the person
I was always destined to be.

Out of the Darkness

The glow of the silvery moon slipped behind a cloud. For a moment the darkness pervaded everywhere. The group huddled closer together, fearful of the darkness; willing the moon to cast its waning light upon them.

The silence surrounding them was broken only by the occasional howling of a dingo or the hoot of an owl. Someone coughed, and another giggled at their collective fear; fear that seemed to bind them together; fear that grew into a cohesive stronghold.

As the moon emerged from its hiding place, shadows were cast upon the ground, appearing grotesque and alive. The nearby bushes rustled as an animal scurried toward its home. The group held their breath; their fear making breathing difficult.

The night was cold and their fire had long since died. No-one had dared leave the camp for firewood. No-one had thought to prepare before darkness fell.

They huddled closer still, praying for the emergence of the early morning light. Each was lost in their own thoughts; their own fears. The purpose of this trip was to connect with the earth. What had seemed like a great idea in the daylight hours—along with confidence and playfulness—had long since dissolved when the sun slid silently behind the mountains.

No planning, no real connection to each other as to who would supply what on this journey; or how they could help and support each other. No-one was prepared for the descending darkness. The night crept into their souls, pulling and tugging at their deepest fears and judgments.

As they sat together thinking silent thoughts; blaming others for the lack of organisation, one person began to sing, quietly at first, tentatively. It didn't take long before another joined in, and then another and another. The song finished and someone had an idea.

'Why don't we work together as a team! Let's stay together and look for firewood. The moon is sharing enough light now for us to see. We will soon be warm if we pull together.' Everyone agreed.

The firewood was quickly gathered and a warming fire thawed the coldest body; the coldest soul. Someone brought out a drum and began to beat a rhythmic beat, a heartbeat. Someone else clapped some of the gathered sticks together, beating in time with the drumming heartbeat. Others clapped on their knees and still others placed their hands on the cool earth. The drumming and clapping seemed to reverberate deep into the earth.

Before long, they began to feel a heartbeat; a pulse coming from the earth. The others stopped drumming and clapping and in the night's silence, they too placed their hands on the earth; they too felt the heart-beat of Mother Earth. Pretty soon, the only sound to be heard was the occasional crackle of the warm fire. Each and every person was con-necting with Mother Earth, as well as to everyone else in the group.

Fear and judgment disintegrated as soul to soul they connected to the oneness of life. Wisdom flowed around that fire that night and well into the next day. No-one spoke; no-one needed to speak. The experience was beyond words.

As they packed up their camp the next morning to leave, each person knew that their lives had changed forever, for the better. They knew that fear could never be present when they connected to the heartbeat and wisdom of the earth. They felt humbled and blessed. They would all live ordinary lives in extraordinary ways!

This would not be the last time that fear and judgement would appear in their darkest of nights, but the wisdom they had learned about themselves at a deep soul level would always guide them out of the dark-ness and into their light.

Pond Life

'Why do you look so tired and unhappy, frog?' asked dragonfly.

'Because there is so much to do,' replied the frog.

'There is no time to be like you, dragonfly. Flying about, dipping here, soaring there. I... have a pond to run,' frog said. 'I have lily pads to sort. I have to make sure everyone sings the same chorus in our environment. I have to make sure that the fish filter the water correctly. I have to make sure the birds don't sit too long in the trees above the pond. I have to make sure the animals who visit don't drink too much of our water.'

'Someone has to do it,' he explained as he puffed out his froggy chest a little more.

'But frog,' said dragonfly, 'we all have our own song to sing and if you take some time to notice, we already sing in harmony with our surroundings. We all have our part to play in our little pond. You don't need to control anything. You don't need to tell any of us how to be... well... ourselves...'

'But I do,' blustered frog. 'Who will keep the pond clean?'

'Who will tell the other animals, insects and birds how to behave around our pond?'

'Why frog, you have taken rather a lot on yourself haven't you?' murmured dragonfly.

'Someone has to do it,' replied frog gruffly.

Dragonfly dipped a little closer and quietly said, 'frog, dear frog, it is not your responsibility to tell all of us who call this pond home, how to be ourselves. We all have a role to play in keeping our home clean and how to make it a fun, safe place for us all to get along.'

Dragonfly waited a moment before saying, 'frog, let go, and enjoy life... as a frog...'

'But…' frog began to stutter, 'who am I if I don't control pond life?'

'You will be one of us, frog,' said dragonfly kindly. 'You will be part of the pond community doing what we do in pond life. You will be happy simply being a frog.'

The Storyteller

The storyteller stood in the centre of the circle of children, a sentinel of knowledge and wisdom. To the children he appeared older than time itself. The lines around his twinkling eyes indicated a lifetime of laughter which belied the serious and urgent tone in his voice.

The children stared at him with rapt attention; each of them mesmerised with his storytelling. He stopped mid-sentence; the children held their collective breath, eager for the next piece of wisdom, the culmination of his story.

Just beyond the circle of children sat a group of parents, each just as eager as their children to hear the final words. They leaned forward, waiting for the happy ending. The silence was only broken by the shallow breathing of the listeners.

The storyteller looked around the circle and beyond. He let the anticipation build. His story was a personal story, a telling of the old ways of the world, a time where flow and change reigned supreme. He told of heroes and heroines, children and old ones. He interspersed a sprinkling of love and courage, always in the face of change. He was a master storyteller. That was his lineage.

He told his stories as though they were ancient stories of times long past. He enthralled his audiences, young and old alike. He had a knack of touching people's hearts and souls. He garnered the complete attention of those around him, taking them on a journey where each listener believed themselves to be a participant in the story.

The timbre of his voice mesmerised people, a hypnotic tone that completely absorbed them. And so now, they leaned closer still, wanting a satisfactory outcome to their personal story. That is how each of them related to his story, as their story. A happy ending would take them home to their beds, satisfied and content.

He began to walk slowly around the circle of children, looking each one of them in the eye. He looked over the circle to the parents. He was still silent. He held the eagerness of his listeners as though in the palms of his hands.

He raised his arms slowly above his head; each pair of eyes watching his every move lest they miss something. Slowly, he began to lower his arms and as he did, he spoke low and soft.

'This story is your story. A story that is never complete. There is no ending, only transitions and new beginnings. Your story, from this point on, is still being told, still unfolding, always shifting and changing.'

'Each of you here tonight has "heard" their own personal story, told in the manner of the old storytellers. Told to touch each of you personally.'

'You have learned this night that you are always the creator of your own story. You have just heard what you recognised as your own journey; each of you the same and yet different.'

'I cannot tell you how your story ends, because it is your own story and there is no ending. Each of you loved this story as your own and you are your own hero or heroine. A hero or heroine that will always create the path that affords you new learning and experiences.'

The storyteller's arms were now again by his side, drawing to a close the storytelling session.

Silence again. He looked at the children and their parents as they realised that their personal stories were being created in every moment, with every breath.

They gathered around him, thanking him for profoundly awakening each of them to their own personal story, affording them an understanding of their position within their own stories.

Each of them, right down to the smallest child, understood that theirs was a never-ending story. A story that changes every time they remember that they *are* the hero or heroine in their own story. This was personal. All other stories flow in harmony with one another to become part of the greater story of life.

They moved away from the storyteller and blended back into their everyday lives, their new awakening expanding into a new story, another new beginning.

Corporate Success

The judge had issued an order. Bankruptcy. How would I ever survive the humiliation of defeat? Where was there left to go, but straight to the bottom?

It all began two years ago when I had a brilliant idea that I could start my own business. I wanted to keep it small; start from home and eventually have a small outlet for my work. A hobby, really.

What happened? My ego!

My family and friends said, 'start big. your idea is unique. It'll work.' My inner voice was saying 'start small, your idea is unique. It'll take time to catch on.'

Who was right? The niggling little voice urging me to start slowly or my family and friends who knew me so well.

That's where my ego kicked in – and how!

Pushing that little voice aside, I rented the biggest premises I could. I went into debt and waited for the orders to pile in. The phone rang occasionally, but more out of curiosity about the product I was selling.

My inner voice grew stronger – pull out while you still can.

My family and friends said 'of course it's going to be slow to begin with, give it time. Don't be impatient. Hang in there.'

So, I again ignored the voice. My family and friends must be right, I'll keep trying.

By the second year, I was losing money hand over fist. I kept borrowing more and more money to stay afloat. I thought that if I got just one big order; one lucky break, I could get myself out of debt.

My family and friends shook their heads. 'Why did you take our advice?' they asked. 'What would we know?' They fell away, one by one; in essence, they deserted me.

Now here I was standing outside bankruptcy court with no money, no home, nowhere to go. I decided to walk awhile – after all, I no longer had a car.

Where was I heading? My feet carried me forward, I didn't care where. I kept my head down and looked at the pavement. I couldn't have lifted my head if I tried.

I had stopped walking. I hadn't realised there were two pairs of feet in my line of vision. One pair was obviously mine; the other pair unknown. Worn runners facing me. I slowly looked up and met the gentlest face and the bluest eyes I had ever seen. I began to cry and the elderly lady opposite me reached out her hand and laid it upon my shoulder.

'Come inside,' she said. 'We've been waiting for you.' I was so miserable; I didn't even register the remark at first. I let her lead me inside an old, dilapidated building.

I had to blink several times to get used to the different light. You see, inside this building was a scene which defies description. The room was filled with a beautiful glow, and I immediately felt an overwhelming sense of peace. This was something I had not had in a long, long time.

There were several people wandering about, taking their time as though they didn't have a care in the world. There was a magnificent pool of water directly in front of me. It sparkled in the light, beckoning me.

I quickly removed my clothes and entered the warm water. As I floated, I felt the trauma and humiliation and defeat disappear to be replaced with hope, love, and determination. I could see my elderly benefactor smile a knowing smile. Her eyes actually twinkled at me. 'This is the healing pool,' she said 'you may come here whenever you wish.' I smiled back at her and closed my eyes as I continued to float.

Sometime later, I opened my eyes, but instead of the healing pool, I found myself lying in my bed. I was disappointed. It was only a dream, I thought, but then my bedroom was filled with the same beautiful glow I had seen in the building. I heard a voice say, 'your reality is your heart, accept the gift of healing as *your* reality and know that success is measured only by what is *in* your heart'.

A Better Day

I am loving and loved
I do my best
I *stand* in the bloody test
Not my fault
No-one to blame

All is a lesson
That we are different
Not the same

There is no falseness in learning
In recognising the journey
Surrendering the yearning

Stripped bare to our very soul
We see our inner light burning
A promise of better tomorrows

Tears fall
Untouched by anything but our emotional heart
Falling at our feet
Watering the earth
New seeds; new life
Growth from a lesson lived and learned

We sheath our sword
The fight over for another round

Weariness tucks us in
'Sleep well little one
Tomorrow is another day ~
A better day full of hope and promise'

Speak Out

In the light of the dawn
On this brand-new day
I open my heart
It's time to have my say

Silence is not an option
Those days are long gone
I will speak and be heard
Discovering where I belong

Words can heal
Words can also destroy
But speaking my truth
Is the tool to employ

Silent words held within
Damaged my soft heart
I know my tribe will listen
Without judgement on their part

Justice will be served
Because my tribe has my back
Taking a deep breath now
I step firmly along my track

I face forward and challenge
What's pushed me to my knees
Because silence near destroyed me
But strength now will be my ease

The first step to healing
Is to speak out and begin
The journey of my worth
I own it now…. because I bloody-well win.

The Timekeeper

How do you keep time?
It's a strange concept—keeping time
When time can't be kept...
Nature herself keeps perfect time
If only we choose to follow her lead
Time appears to rule our everyday lives
And yet...
We can stretch time
We can stop time
We can manipulate time to suit our needs
Our personal growth moves us onto new timelines
Always changing
Always stretching us from one timeline to another
Keeping time is man-made
Time itself is made up of sunrises and sunsets and everything in
    between
It's new moons and full moons
Waxing and waning
Altering tidal flows
It's the seasons rolling ever onward
Regardless of how we choose to fill our time
The Ancients moved with nature's time cycles
Until the clock took precedence over nature
How we work with time is significant
We are the timekeepers—the clock watchers...
What if... every waking moment wasn't asking us to be a slave to time?

What if… we looked at time like we look at our finances to see where
   we can cut back to create more?

What if… we sifted through our minutes and decided where we can
   reclaim time?

How would that look?

Would you sit awhile and relax into those reclaimed moments?

Or create something beautiful?

Or fill reclaimed time with another busy?

We have a choice how to fill time

We… are the timekeepers…

But nature is the one who teaches us that time is more than a clock…

Be Present

My future is guaranteed
As long as I am present
In my present.
My past is a memory
My future is my potential.
I choose to live now
And not miss a single moment
Of my wonderful life.

I Am Me

I am me as I am
Not who I wish to be
I am perfect as I am
Not a shadow of someone else
I have wisdom
I have trust
I have faith, truth and love
I am all I need to be
After all I am me!

Grace

In silence comes wisdom
In wisdom comes truth
In truth comes integrity
In integrity comes Grace

Fulfillment

Grace & Beauty
Serenity & Light
These are aspects
Which are inherent within you
Hold your head high
Respect your inner guidance
And stride forward
With purpose and confidence
In every step you take
Toward eternal fulfillment

Colour My World Rainbow

I'm blind. Legally blind. Have been since the day I was born. I've never seen a tree. I've never read a book. I've never seen your face. And yet, I know what a tree looks like. I know the words in books and I know your face.

I sense everything and pictures form in my mind. The one thing that has always frustrated me was colour. How does one run their hands over colour and know what it is? How does one 'see' colour in their mind's eye?

This was my one wish in life. To know colour. I didn't let it get me down, but some days, I would be wistful and wonder what colour was like.

One day, I was taking my dog Rusty to a nearby park. It had been raining and everything smelled fresh. The grass, the soil, the air had all been washed clean. I could feel the weak sunshine on my face as we walked side by side.

I sensed someone was watching us but was hesitant to approach. We kept walking, but the sensation of someone near to us was persistent. We stopped, and I asked, 'Does someone wish to speak to me?'

The person came forward and touched my arm. It was a small child, and she asked 'Mister, can you see rainbows?'

'No,' I answered, 'I cannot see rainbows'.

'That's a pity,' she said, 'because you are standing right in the middle of one. You should make a wish.'

Well, as you can imagine, I was pretty excited at the thought of standing in a rainbow and almost without thinking, I wished I could see it. Suddenly, new sensations appeared and things I had never before experienced happened. I could 'see'. See with my inner eyes.

I *knew* which colour was red. I *knew* which was blue, which was violet and yellow and all of the other colours of the rainbow. I could feel the vibration of each and every one of them. They were all different and yet cohesive in their togetherness.

I realised that these sensations had been a part of me my whole life but it took a child to show me how to colour my world rainbow.

The Garden

A burst of colour
Fragrance in the air
A deep breath now
And a smile we will share

Spring brings warmth
And cool nights too
With ink black nights
Awakening a whole new view

My garden grows love
Through plants and trees
With pathways that meander
To wander as I please

Silver birch and gum trees
Roses and lavender too
Are just some of the joys
Shared with me and you

Tea in my garden
Under a canopy of green
A new day dawning
That magic of the in-between

Neither night-time nor day
Gentle stillness prevails
Not a breath of wind stirs
As we balance the old scales

There is something precious
Sitting in a garden drinking tea
To share life's bounty
For one and all to see

One step and then three
I step onto wild thyme
Breathing in the aroma
So fresh and sublime

The birds say good morning
A song of sacred cheer
They greet the new day
Devoid of all fear

I take my lessons
In this place I revere
It's mystical qualities
Chase away *all* my fear

I begin *my* new day
With peace in my heart
Tea in my garden
Offers a brand-new start

The Portal

I watch from my window as the deer and the kangaroos, the wallabies and the wombats, walk into the forest. One by one, they disappear from my view. The fringe of the forest is a magical place, you see. An egress from one world to another. I haven't been there but I know it to be so as I have often watched this melding of animals and forest from my window. Each animal knows the exact point where the landscape manipulates what humans consider reality. Shapeshifters of time and place.

Before the last of the animals have stepped across the threshold into invisibility, I race from my viewing place and into the wilds of the forest. There I see a shimmering gateway, a portal of some sort, that sparks with light for a moment as the final animal steps through and begins to fade from sight.

Without thought for mind and limb, I leap through the fading shimmering light. Surprisingly, I land lightly on my feet.

The scene around me is the same and yet different. More vibrant, more alive somehow. There are three things I notice on my arrival at this magical place. The first thing is the beautiful silence. It's not an empty silence, but rather a place of opportunity to *feel* into the silence. What a strange concept. A place where everyday thoughts don't matter as much as the feeling all around me that scooped me up in a loving embrace, as it planted seeds of ideas within my heart and mind at the same time. The silence is filled with possibilities beyond human understanding.

The second thing is the added layer of light. I gaze around me and see that the light is emanating with pulsing fractals from the trees, from the earth itself and from the cerulean sky above me. It seemed to me to be a way of experiencing life beyond ordinary vision. This pulsing energy filled me with patterns unlike anything I had ever experienced.

So far, what I could hear and see was amplified beyond my other everyday world.

The third thing I noticed was how I was feeling. I was feeling intense healing energies, like all my ailments were dissolving into nothingness. I looked down at my body and saw that it was luminescent. I was glowing with good health and it showed. I was actually not my physical body now. I was simply light.

Time didn't appear to exist. This mystical place exists beyond time.

I began to walk along a path that felt soft and warm under my feet, energising me with every step I took.

The animals I had watched from my window as they entered this special place emerged from the trees. I could see their own luminescent bodies. They watched my progression through the forest curiously.

Nothing seemed solid. It was all just pure energy that I experienced effortlessly through all of my senses. I felt marvellous. I felt contented.

I watched the animals as they began to return to the gateway. It started to shimmer again as the first one stepped across the threshold and stepped back into the everyday world. I could see through the shimmer and witnessed the animals return to their physical forms. Each one seemed livelier than they had before they entered the forest.

The last ones were ready to cross back into the world in which I lived my everyday life. I followed them back through this gateway and stood at the edge of this forest. I felt alive in my world with more energy than I had experienced in a very long time.

Interestingly, thoughts began to return but with less negative impact than before. The external noise was pure magic as I listened to the breeze in the canopy of the forest, and the birds chattered away as they looked for grubs below the surface of the earth. I could hear more. The light around me was a little more vibrant. I felt something had shifted within my physical body. It didn't ache as much. My heart beat a little slower, my breathing was less laboured. I was much more present to the heightened vibrations of what was around me in my physical world environment.

I could see that the forest or indeed any forest held the secrets of wellbeing. Animals knew it, and each day undertook a pilgrimage of sorts to rejuvenate their own energy bodies.

Today I learned that stepping outside of my own comfort zone, that I thought was my window to the world, shows me that entering into the unknown can bring mystical and significant experiences that we can apply to life…. everyday life.

I feel rejuvenated because I followed the lead of the animals around me and stepped into a forest of mystery.

My quest now is to follow a path of self-discovery and healing by following the leads nature provides. There is more to experience in life when we step outside the door of comfort into nature's magic.

Earth's Song

Mountains so tall
You inspire me to climb
Valleys so deep
You encourage me to explore
Rivers flowing
I surrender to wisdom's song
Oceans so vast
I dream on your stormy waves
Earth my mother
My grandmother
And soul keeper
You keep me on track
When chaos strikes my heart
Fire my passion
Air my wings
Water my tears
Earth my anchor
My humanness is my purpose
My wholeness to shine
I climb my tallest mountains
Explore my deepest valleys
And float on wisdom's song
Dreaming the big dreams
Because
I live
I live
I live

Until my final breath
And still, I live on
In the hearts of songs of love
A bard of tribal stories
Connected through earth's heartbeat
Until the next round
When we will meet again

Colour Your World With Rainbows

Colour your world with rainbows
And experience joy
Beyond your wildest dreams
Rainbows are your soul experience
They are your reason for living;
Your reason for loving.
Acknowledge the rainbow within you
Say hello to the rainbow around you
Feel peace in your soul
Feel love in your heart
We *are* living rainbows
And we *are* the perfection of rainbows complete

Touch a Rainbow

When you touch a rainbow
You put your hand upon your heart
Each and every colour
Resonates with the loving person within
Each and every colour
Determines our path in life
So, touch a rainbow today
And allow the journey to begin;
Not at the beginning
But as a continuation of the path we have followed
For an eternity

Behold Life

A tree is but a tree
Until we truly behold its beauty.
A sky is but a sky
Until we truly behold its colour.
A river is but a river
Until we truly behold its majesty.
A bird is but a bird
Until we truly behold its voice.
What do we learn from this?
To truly behold – Life!

There're Weeds in My Garden

There're weeds in my garden

I think it's a mess
Too much to assess
Not enough care
Leaves scattered everywhere

There're weeds in my garden

It's too overwhelming
My fear is not helping
It's a challenge too far
How high do I set the bar?

There're weeds in my garden

I can't stand to see them
I just want to condemn them
To close the bloody door
'Cause there's more weeds than before

There're weeds in my garden

I see the metaphor
But it's all been said before
But I'll state in my case
That tomorrow… I'll face that mighty place

Sigh

There're weeds in my garden

My grandma would see seeds
She wouldn't see any weeds
She'd acknowledge their place
And see no disgrace

There're weeds in my garden

She would say plant more flowers
Before your fear overpowers
Please sow your good deeds
in amongst the many weeds

There're weeds in my garden

I see them as needy
These stories I deem weedy
But they are part of who I am
So what... I don't give a damn

There're weeds in my garden

My grandma calls them gems
She says simply love them
Share space with my weeds
Because they *all* begin with seeds

There're weeds in my garden

I can now see their worth
They're all part of this earth
So I scatter flowers amongst my weeds
Let's see where this story leads

There're weeds in my garden

They no longer bother me
The notion sets me free
There's always space amongst the weeds
To plant beautiful flower seeds

There're weeds in my garden

Painful stories healed by seeds
Flowers growing now amongst the weeds
Stories made true and whole
Within the sanctity of my very own soul

There're weeds in my garden

The animals visit to feed
Not discerning flowers from weed
Wisdom called in... for one final note
So for now dear readers... it's *all* she wrote

Wild Spaces

Wild spaces make my heart sing,
In anticipation
With awe
In deep respect for what Mother Earth shares with us

It's a cottage garden
It's the wildness of the sea
It's a forest green and quiet
And a waterfall when the sun catches its spray to create the magic of
    dancing rainbows

It's snow-capped mountains
And the sound a stream makes as it meanders elegantly over smooth
    rocks

Wild spaces live in my heart
A treasure trove of wonder secreted away
As reminders for the days when the outside natural world is elusive

Wild spaces
We all have them
They exist as markers so that we explore our natural world… often…
So we remember what it's like to simply breathe… nature

Into the Secret Garden

Into the secret garden
A delightful space to be
Not a time to rush ahead
It's quite simply the place for me

Into the secret garden
A paradise of green on green
With magical places and simple spaces
There is simply no need for routine

Into the secret garden
A place where mystery dwells
Imaginarium with eyes wide open
Dreaming thoughts of magic and spells

Into the secret garden
Where one can hold no pretences
A world on its own has called to me
There's no need to come to my senses

Into the secret garden
Time willingly lost into the now
The fairies have called and asked me
If I would take a heart-warming vow

Into the secret garden
A wise woman stands and waits
For me to say the words
That will seal my loving fate

Into the secret garden
I come with my heart on my sleeve
I vow to tend my garden
A sanctuary for all who believe

Into the secret garden
A place for young and old
With innocent eyes to see what's there
Taking steps on pathways of gold

Into the secret garden
A place of many faces
You only need your heart to look
And it will take you many places

Into the secret garden
A place where the wise woman lives
Her knowledge, grace and wisdom
Is for her alone to give

Into the secret garden
A place of secrets and mystery
A feel-good space in this chaotic world
Where your experience is your victory

Medicine Walk

Walk the medicine walk
Heed the medicine talk
The natural world is calling.

She offers up many clues
To take plant-based medicines
To eat food as medicine
To stretch our body
To breathe fresh air
To connect with the spirits of place
To open our heart to love for our natural spaces
Challenging our mind to heal
So that we may step into good health
To the best of our ability
One curious but compelling footfall at a time.

She offers herself to all of us,
In all her healing ways.

It's a choice we will make throughout our lifetime;
accepting her gifts of life affirming worth and healing miracles.
As always… her healing healthy ways will soothe the spirit within us all.

Wisdom of the Ages

The wisdom of the ages
Is there for all to see
A light in the tunnel
A time now to be free

Sacred keys to unlock
The most difficult of doors
You will find that love
Is the only way to stop wars

The wisdom of the ages
Offers a unique way of life
Shared by our ancestors
Who lived in the light

The dark times came
And their light still shone bright
A spark of great hope
Handed down through the fight

The old ones believed
In the generations to come
That a day would arrive
When their vision would be done

They drummed through the years
Beating Mother Earth's song
The rhythm would be heard
In the hearts of the strong

Today and tomorrow
The messages will be heard
Love is the answer
The true and honest word

Shine your light for the lost
May they find their way home
To a pathway of love
Wherever they choose to roam

Brothers and sisters
All across our earth
Holding hands in the dark
Will see a collective re-birth

In this time of war and strife
Be the candle flickering bright
Just as night turns to day
Dark times becomes light

It begins with one candle
Shining light in the dark
One becomes thousands
All from one spark

You *are* the one spark
The way onward is clear
One spark or one voice
Will chase away naked fear

Breathe Life

Walk in the sunshine, dance in the moonlight
Look up to the stars and down to the earth
Wriggle your toes over the dewy morning grass
Roll down the hill
Plunge into the cold sea
Never be old of mind and heart.
Live… love
Embrace trees
Lay over rocks
Jump rope
Tell stories
Be quiet… be loud… as the mood dictates.
Whisper the songs in your heart to the mountains
Chant in the caves
Laugh at absurdities
Cry at sad stories
Think sanguine thoughts.
There is now… and then there is now… There is *only* now…
Be all that you are…
For we are here for a moment, a breath, a memory
Until we sleep the long sleep of peace
Our final breath taking the memories we made in a lifetime into our
    soul
To be remembered next time we live… we love…
Breathe… life into life
There is only now!

The Space Between

There comes a time
In everyone's life
When they must enter the space between.
You know what I mean
The space
That creates the pause on life
For a little while
Perhaps a longer while.
That space
Where stillness is necessary
To heal
To grow
To see a new view.
You may think
Nothing happens
In the space between
And yet
It is a space
Where your imagination can soar
Learning how to fly
To create
To love deeply.
The space between
Is for quiet contemplation
A space to dance
To your heart's music.
Nothing to do

Nowhere to be
A place to simply
Breathe
And be free.

Who Am I?

Who am I but the wind?

Who am I but the gentle flowing river?

Who am I but the white wispy clouds meandering in the clear skies above?

Who am I but the vibrant colours of the rainbow?

Who am I but a majestic eagle in flight?

Who am I but a pebble in the pond of life?

Who am I – really?

I am my own creative self – capable of creating my own destiny; fulfilling my life purpose with grace and truth.

I am mother, grandmother, wife, lover and friend.

I am all of these things;

I am part of the oneness of all life's creation.

But most importantly – I am me!

We Are

We are the fire that ignites passion for life's journey

We are the air that breathes life into new adventures

We are the free-flowing water that nourishes the earth wherever we
    may journey

We are the earth that anchors all that is needed

We are the stars that guide the way

We are whole

We are perfect as we are

We are life

We are the Wise Women

Fire… Earth … Air… Water and Stars

Unite us now

We are one

Blessed Be

The Teacup

The teacup had sat on the woman's shelf of treasures for many years. It was a delicate flowered piece that had been handed down through many generations of women in her family. It was beautiful to some, but the woman often thought of just throwing it away. It was full of chips and cracks and leaked whenever tea was poured into it. It showed the worn-out signs of attempted repairs over its long lifetime.

The woman was dusting the shelf on which it sat one day when memories began to flow into her. She saw images in her mind of the teacup sitting on her mother's kitchen table and before that, it had proudly sat on her grandmother's table. It had only been for decoration though, as it leaked tea all over the table. The woman could still remember the laughter this ancient teacup evoked, and she smiled at the memories. She remembered this fractured and broken teacup being handed around the table with each woman present sharing a story of their own. It didn't seem to matter that the teacup couldn't be filled with tea. It was filled with stories instead.

It was all part of the ritual of sitting at the kitchen table with laughter and tears and story sharing. It was part of the remembering and hon-ouring of those who came before as it was passed from hand to hand.

The woman's mother had given the teacup to her long ago, telling her that it was so old that no-one could remember a time when it *wasn't* on the table at special women's gatherings.

The woman couldn't really see the point, as it didn't seem to have much purpose in her modern-day world. She didn't hold gatherings like her mother and grandmother had done. Life was just too busy, and there didn't seem to be a point to it. Life was so different now to the old days.

She came out of her reverie and realised that she was holding the teacup in her hand. Perhaps that was what had evoked such pleasant memories.

Her mother's words as she handed the teacup reverently to her daughter came back to her. 'This teacup represents all of the stories of all of the women in our family and of all of the friendships formed over a lifetime of sharing stories over tea. There will come a time when your own stories will be added to it. You will know when that time is right. Ultimately it will pass on to your own daughter.'

The woman looked at the cup and remembered the words as though spoken a day ago, an hour ago, a minute ago. She missed her mother's wisdom shared over a cup of tea. She turned the teacup over in her hand and it slipped from her grasp, falling to the floor in seemingly slow motion. She heard her own voice cry out as the teacup shattered into many pieces.

Broken stories littered her floor.

She sank to the floor and sobbed. Her tears created droplets of sadness that fell onto the broken shards. Stories shared over many lifetimes were now lost in the debris.

She wished she had listened more to the stories. She wished she had learned more from the women sharing tea around the kitchen table. She wished she hadn't dismissed the importance of the teacup. Generational stories had been added to the teacup at each sacred gathering, and they were now lying broken around her.

The woman heard her mother's voice in her heart. 'Mend the teacup and add your own stories. Mend it with love and make it strong. Hear the old stories in your heart. Share the teacup with other women in your life, your daughter, your friends. *Make* the time to share stories with laughter and tears around your own kitchen table. It's not the teacup itself that is important, but what it represents. It's the connection of women over tea, feeling safe and secure in that time and place, sharing as only women can share. *This* is what this old teacup represents. Mend it. The next chapter is written in all of the teacups shared with the women you love.'

The woman smiled as she gathered the pieces of the teacup. She knew her own new chapter had begun and it's all thanks to an ancient chipped, fractured and currently broken teacup. The pieces will form a new beginning, and it is her turn to share stories... with love.

That's the magic of the teacup. It's the spark of sharing over a cup of tea.

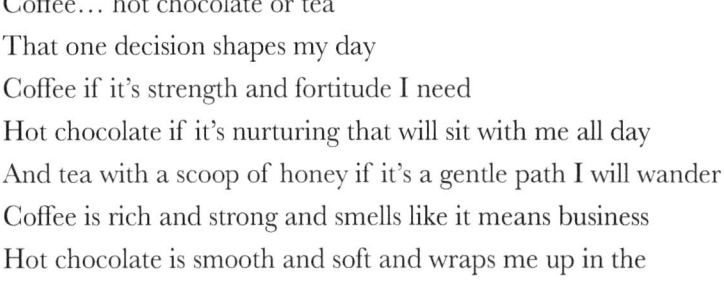

Coffee… Hot Chocolate or Tea

Coffee… hot chocolate or tea
That one decision shapes my day
Coffee if it's strength and fortitude I need
Hot chocolate if it's nurturing that will sit with me all day
And tea with a scoop of honey if it's a gentle path I will wander
Coffee is rich and strong and smells like it means business
Hot chocolate is smooth and soft and wraps me up in the
    mmmmmmm
Tea is my thinking drink when I am moving into a space to create
To write
To mould clay
To have my hands in the earth…

Mix It Up

To explore the next part of your journey
Mix together the following seven ingredients....
Take a deep breath of trust
Add a dollop of change
Include a largish splash of mystery
Stir in a heartfelt wish
Whip in a liberal pinch of wisdom
Add a few generous shakes of truth
And finally
A substantial wedge of deep love....
Stir vigorously all together
And sit in the sun to set
You'll know when it's done
It will rise like a cake
And taste sweet to the senses
The best thing is
It's self-sustaining
Because
Once made
It will never... ever... run out

Dance

Dance on your own
Really… no-one is watching
Cut loose
Dance in the supermarket
Everyone is watching
And they play great tunes
Dance with loved ones around the kitchen table
Dance with strangers when the music gets your feet tapping
Dance to the beat of your own heart
Dance under the moonlight
Barefoot on the grass
But never ever stop the dance
That's where your creative spirit gets his or her spark
That's what opens your heart to joy
Evoking memories
Bringing laughter
Tears sometimes
Love always
Being in the moment
Making new memories
Dance… Dance… dance…

Heart's Rule

The mind is so complex
The heart so simple
Why not let our hearts rule
And let the mind follow

With Love

Everything begins with love
Everything returns to love
What happens between love
Can continue throughout creation and eternity
With love

Transformation

The freedom and beauty
Of the butterfly
Transforms me to encourage
My creativity to flow
Joyfully within me

The Waterfall

I gazed in awe at the majesty of the waterfall before me. Its beauty brought tears to my eyes. Tears which mingled with the spray of the waterfall as it reached my face. I had walked deep into the gully and, although my expectations were high, they did not measure up to Mother Nature's splendour.

Ferns grew on the sides of the cliffs, ledges jutted out, and small caves appeared behind the cascading water. What secrets did these caves hold, I wondered? I felt I was not alone and yet I could not see or hear anyone. It was more of a sensation – a knowing that I was in the presence of someone or something.

I closed my eyes and tried to pinpoint exactly where this sensation was coming from. I relaxed into the sounds of the waterfall. With my eyes closed, I could hear every drop splashing onto the rocks on their way down to the pool below. I could hear birds singing high in the branches of the trees surrounding me.

I could feel a warmth and calm settling through me; bringing peace to my soul which I had not felt in a long, long time. I couldn't remember when I had last felt this good. I tried to capture the serenity of this place with my inner eyes so that I could take it home with me. I didn't want the feeling to end, and I wanted to try and share that feeling with others. I took one last deep, cleansing breath and opened my eyes.

What I saw in front of me made me think that I was dreaming; I must have fallen asleep. Everything around me had changed. It was the same gully, the same waterfall, and yet it was all different. I had stepped into another place and time. My initial fear and surprise were replaced by an inner excitement and anticipation. I had somehow been transported to the realm of fairies and angels, tree spirits and rock faces with eyes, a nose and a mouth. There were birds and animals I had never before seen. They were every rainbow colour imaginable.

A man and woman emerged from the waterfall. They appeared to walk straight through the water and yet they were dry. I didn't dare move as they made their way toward me. I thought that if I moved so much as a muscle that the scene before me would disappear. They were beautiful and I thought that they looked like a matching pair of bookends; the same and yet different. They had a familiarity about them, but I couldn't imagine why.

As they came closer, the man and woman reached out to me and I felt compelled to move forward and grasp their outstretched hands. No-one had spoken and yet I knew their intent and felt their love for our surroundings. They propelled me forward, straight over the pool of water. As we neared the waterfall, I feared I was about to be drenched.

The waterfall suddenly changed and instead of water cascading over us, a rainbow appeared the full length of the rock face. It was so vibrant and alive. We stopped under it for a moment. I felt totally energised by the many colours.

I then looked behind the rainbow and saw an opening. It was enormous and a crystal entrance greeted us. The brilliant glow from the quartz and amethyst was enough to light the way.

Guarding the entrance to the cave were several magnificent beings. They had human bodies, but they also had enormous wings coming straight out from their backs. These wings had patterns and colours on them and, when unfolded, were breathtakingly beautiful. Each one greeted me by enfolding me in their wings. They passed me from one to the other until I found myself deep within the crystal cave.

I still had not dared to speak in case I broke this spell, but I had begun to wonder why I had been blessed with entry to this magical realm. Were all visitors granted access, or was I the only one? Why was I here?

I didn't have to wait long to find out. There in front of me was an enormous golden throne encrusted with crystals of all varieties. Sitting on the throne was a woman. By my judgment, she was quite elderly, but her presence was certainly regal. There was a fire pit in front of her and I moved forward and sat with the fire between us. She needed no words, no actions. I just knew what was required. I bowed my head in acknowledgement and then closed my eyes. I was suddenly very weary. I knew I was dreaming and yet everything that happened was perfectly clear.

I could see myself sitting in front of the fire in the crystal cave and then I was quickly whisked away. The cave disappeared and I was flying way out into the Universe. I *was* the Universe. I was everything that was ever created. I felt wonderful. There was peace and contentment, love, and the feeling that I could go on forever. I was aware that I was here for a reason but I was having too much fun to focus my attention. I flew faster than I ever thought possible. I saw stars being formed; I felt the warmth of the sun. I basked in the glow of many moons from many different planets.

I gradually became aware that I was not alone. The man and woman from the waterfall flanked me on either side. Patience was written all over them as they waited for me to concentrate on what they were trying to show me. I slowed my pace and allowed them to guide me. They smiled serenely and took my hands as we darted off into the void which was directly in front of us. I had not noticed it before which was just as well because I did not have time to be fearful of what lay ahead. What I thought was a black hole was actually brilliant with colours I recognized, and many I did not know. As we passed through each colour, I felt a different emotion. Some were gentle and loving; some were overwhelming in their clarity. As I passed through this particular set of colours, I suddenly knew everything; the answers to all the questions I had ever asked.

I wanted to stay and feel every colour there was, but my friends had other plans. We again took off and headed deeper and deeper into this well of feeling. I felt joy, love, sadness, determination and totally energised. I had never experienced anything like it. A little way ahead, I could see a golden glow. As we drew closer, I realised that this glow was emanating from a large sphere which appeared to float in nothingness. It was continually rotating and as it did, little pinpricks of light were being flicked off the surface.

It was magnificent. I looked at my companions and they nodded their assent to my unasked question. I moved forward with my hand outstretched. As I did this, I could feel denseness; I guessed this sphere had an aura. I moved closer and gently laid my hand upon the surface of the sphere. My hand and arm started to tingle and then my whole body started to shake and glow with golden light. I took my hand away and saw that my imprint had remained on the surface of the sphere.

What did this mean? I turned to ask my two companions, but found I was completely alone. I felt no fear, no apprehension. I smiled to myself and reached toward the sphere. I giggled softly as I was again embraced in the tingling sensation. What a place! What an experience!

I knew without a shadow of a doubt that I had just reached out to the very soul of my being; the imprint of everything I am – known and unknown. This was my blueprint – it possessed knowledge about my past, my present and my future. I knew with clarity my direction, my journey. This experience was filled with a deep concentrated love of which I cannot describe. I had touched my universe, my essence. I had thus far survived the journey of my life and would survive for all eternity. This time I laughed out loud and I could hear the echo bounce around the colours surrounding me and engulfing me in pure joy. My inner child was free. Free at last to express herself without fear of punishment or reprisal.

Just at that moment, a beautiful white horse cantered toward me and nuzzled my face with his. I instinctively knew he was there to take me wherever I wanted or needed to go. I didn't want this to end. I just wanted to keep experiencing the world beyond where I lived. This was the reality I truly wanted for myself.

As soon as these thoughts escaped, I knew them to be selfish, and I found myself hurtling back to the crystal cave.

No, I silently cried. I don't want to go back.

I opened my eyes and the woman on the throne finally spoke. 'When you allow thoughts free reign, you can access anything, anytime and any-where. You can live comfortably in both realms, physical and spiritual. When you control your thoughts, you limit yourself and find yourself frustrated in your desires. Look behind you,' she said.

I did as I was told and there in all of his magnificence was the white horse. He walked over and nuzzled into my hair. I was overjoyed to see him.

'He is always with you child. He will take you to your freedom of spirit.'

'Remember to relinquish control of your journey and allow people and events to happen freely. When you do this, you let the beauty of existence enter your life. His name is Shekile. Honour him and call to him in your dreams.'

I was just about to open my mouth to speak when I was again whisked away. This time, on the back of my white horse. I was overjoyed. We appeared to be flying across the surface of a large body of water, an ocean. The sun was shining reflectively on the horizon, casting golden ripples the length and breadth of this ocean.

A small island came into view. It rose high above the sea in a single mountain top. Shekile was heading straight for this island. As we galloped closer, I could see a beautiful temple glowing with gold and silver hues sitting at the very top of the mountain. There was someone waving at us. I couldn't believe it. She was smiling at us as though she was expecting us. She was beautiful. Tall and slender, with long silver hair. She was dressed medieval style in the palest of pinks, blues and mauves. Her eyes glowed silver, the same as her hair. We came to a halt just in front of her and as I dismounted she came to me and embraced me.

She softly called my name and welcomed me to her home. She turned and bowed to Shekile and beckoned me to follow her. We entered the temple through huge crystal doors. The room we entered was enormous, but totally devoid of furniture. There was a vast glass dome ceiling in the centre of the room. The floor was inlaid with gold and silver and embedded with crystals. These were set out in intricate patterns with a large centre circle underneath the dome.

The woman drew me to the centre of the circle and turned to face me. 'I am Gaia, the ethereal essence of Mother Earth. It is here that we teach the connection between Heaven and Earth. This dome reflects the sun, the moon and the stars. It brings together the earth keepers. We meet on the dark moon and again on the full moon. The full moon is one of creativity and much can be achieved through global activation.'

Tonight, is the first full moon of the New Year. The energies of the four directions will be joining us, as well as representatives of every living entity of this earth. We invoke the will of the Universe through combining the loving energies of everyone present. We help this great planet create new awareness, new thought processes, new clarity, and new ideas. You are here as a representative of the human race. Your loving heart has brought you to us. You will sit by my right hand and be open to the physical presence of all humanity.

I was overwhelmed by all that I had heard, but at the same time proud that I had been chosen to represent humanity. It would be several hours before everyone gathered together under the full moon and Gaia had instructed me to familiarise myself with everything on the island. I went back outside and sat myself at the very edge of a cliff. There was so much to take in and I wondered how I could help in the creative processes of Earth. Could the power of love really be enough to change what was happening to Earth?

I had so many unanswered questions. Would there still be war? Would there still be abuse? Would there still be poverty and hunger? Would there still be jealousy and anger? I couldn't imagine a world which would instantly change. I sat watching the beautiful blue sea and the equally blue sky. The scene before me was totally devoid of any other colour. Is it any wonder I felt so calm and relaxed in my body. Gradually the questions in my mind slowed until there were no questions – no thoughts. I was totally at one with the cliffs and the sky and the sea.

I don't know how long I sat there, but I eventually realised that the sun was low on the horizon and that directly in line with it in the opposite direction was the moon. If I held out both hands, I felt I could hold each of them. I would be in total balance, with this island as the centre of my being.

It came to my mind that I could indeed do this. I stood on the edge of the cliff face and stretched a hand in either direction. I could see the reflection of the sun going down in my left hand. It glowed red and gold and tingled with warm energy. As I looked at my right hand, the palm glowed with silver and gold and again felt warm, which was a surprise to me. I had thought the feeling would be cool. I looked straight ahead and as I did this, I felt my centre as each part of me blended together in total harmony. There was such a feeling of overwhelming emotion. Love filled every cell of my human form. I was now in balance and ready to begin whatever was about to happen.

I walked back through the crystal doors and was surprised to see the domed room was full of different entities. Some I could recognise, many I could not. There were hundreds of us. Gaia beckoned to me to take my place by her side. She turned to me and said, 'I hear your questions. Tonight, many will be answered, and some will disappoint you. You have expectations. All humanity has expectations. Release them and allow only the loving energy from your soul to flow freely without restriction. We will now begin.'

Everyone was assembled around the circle and silence prevailed as we all sat cross-legged on the floor. The only light in the room was the glow of the full moon as it ascended in the night sky. No words were spoken – everyone knew what to do. I took three deep breaths to relax and decided to take my cues from Gaia on my left, and an angel sitting to my right. I began to hear sounds, and all at once I realised that musical notes were floating to my ears. I wondered where they were coming from. There was no-one playing any instruments.

I sat quietly and tried to clear my head but I was beginning to feel light headed and was having trouble remaining focused. I was becoming separated from my physical body and as I looked around, every single entity was doing exactly the same thing; all gently floating above their bodies. Not only that, but I could see into their hearts. Their hearts glowed gold and white. I looked down at my heart and it too was open and glowing.

Immediately the music reached a crescendo and the gold and white began to swirl around this floating circle. It was like a beautiful vortex taking every loving feeling with it. It was still swirling furiously when the moon appeared at the uppermost part of the dome and shone directly into the centre of our circle.

The music abruptly stopped and the silence was total. The gold and white vortex peaked and returned to the hearts of everybody in the circle. I looked down to where the moonlight shone at the centre of the circle. Movement caught my eye. The centre section of the floor was gently raised toward us as we floated above our bodies. It was like the moon was the key to unlocking the secrets of the world. Then I realised that this was indeed true. The moon was the key to everything.

As this illuminated platform continued upward, I could see someone standing in the centre; it was Gaia. I had thought she was still sitting to my left. I quickly glanced in this direction and saw that she had left a space for her return. I looked back. Her arms were lifted high above her head, reaching to the moon. She was singing a song I did not understand and yet it tugged at my heart. It tugged at the hearts of everyone. Gold and white intertwined cords reached out to her until she could gather them together. She held them to the moonlight and as she continued singing, we merged with the full moon. Our hearts became one, and I felt love for every single entity in this room. The moon continued on its way, making its slow descent to the other side of the earth.

I had now returned to my physical body and Gaia was again seated to my left. There were no walls, no barriers between any of us. Our questions had been answered, our hearts had been permanently opened to give and receive love from this great planet.

I knew that I was now a key to awakening people to their inner light. It was my journey to take light to humanity, and it was the journey of others in the room to take light to their kind. I learned that we are all light; we just need to find the light switch. I also learned that there would still be wars, and there would still be anger and jealousy.

However, as we touch just one other person, the earth becomes a lighter place. I turned to face Gaia, and she took me into her arms and rocked me like a child. She then stepped back and her silver eyes gazed directly into mine.

'The night is over and you have achieved the right to deliver light to humanity. This will be done by keeping the flame of love which resides in your heart alight at all times. You do not need to do anything special; you do not need to preach words. Just be yourself and share your love unconditionally. We will meet again. Go with my love and the love of all your companions here tonight. Farewell.'

I bowed my head and kissed her hands and then turned and walked out through the crystal doors to the waiting Shekile. He nuzzled my face and as I mounted him, I turned for one last look at this magical island, but it was already fading from my vision like a beautiful dream.

We returned to the cave. I should have been very weary but I was totally invigorated. I was told that they had one more journey for me to complete before I returned to the world of my kind. I sensed the presence of my two guides. I turned to them and bowed in recognition. They came forward and again flanked me on either side.

The ground under my feet rumbled and began to open. I jumped back in fear, but my guides urged me forward. Trust, I heard in my mind. So, trust I did and took a big leap of faith forward and began hurtling toward the centre of the earth. It was completely black and yet I felt no fear. I knew that blackness is the void where creativity is born, not unlike the female womb.

I could pinpoint a glimmer of light. I did not know which way was up, so I could not find a direction for it. The pinpoint began to grow. The closer I became, the brighter the glow. I had to turn my head, because the light was hurting my eyes.

I stopped suddenly and landed gracefully on my feet. As my eyes adjusted to the light, I realised that I was indeed at the centre of the earth. What I was seeing was breathtaking. A city of light and crystal surrounded me. My eyes pricked with tears at the sight of a city thought lost. Atlantis was alive and well, in the core of Mother Earth.

A woman was walking toward me with both arms outstretched to embrace me. She looked grandmotherly and weathered with time. Her eyes were so soft and gentle; I felt I was melting into them. I returned her embrace and kissed her cheeks tenderly. I had come home. I was welcome here and accepted. This woman is the earthly essence of our great mother. She is the keeper of faith and hope. Her city is working constantly to keep light shining to the surface. This light is then blended with the light of the Universe and love is born. It is instilled in the hearts of every human being.

Many feel and experience the love of our cosmic parents. Others push it all aside as they feel that to love, is to be vulnerable. I became aware that we all have the ability to give and receive an enormous amount of love, however only some may recognise it in this lifetime.

This wonderful lady took me to a crystal lake which shone brightly with the clearest water I had ever seen. We sat at the water's edge and allowed the water to lap at our feet. Quartz crystals filled with rainbows and complete little cities within each one appeared to me. Each had a story to tell. Each was eager to show me their loving work. These crystals eventually make their way to the surface of this planet to be found by people who need their loving support. My purpose is to teach people to open their awareness to the beauty of crystals.

This was yet another magical place I never wanted to leave. I had never before known that earth contained such inner beauty and knowledge. We just need to know how to access it. I will return here many times in my lifetime. Each time, I will discover something new to share with others who are willing to learn and grow. Little by little, we expand our horizons beyond the mundane to live the extraordinary life of blending our spiritual selves with our physical selves. It is possible for the human race to survive the holocaust of self-destruction.

I closed my eyes for a moment to offer thanks for this journey and when I opened them, I was again in the cave. This time I was alone. There was not much light and the only sound was the waterfall at the entrance of the cave. I looked around but could find no evidence of my new friends. The cave did not glow with the brilliance of crystals. I began to wonder whether I had perhaps stumbled and hit my head. Maybe these happenings had all been a beautiful dream. It made me sad to think that they were not real.

I moved forward to find my way out of the cave. I reached out my hand to steady myself on the rocky surface and as I did, my hand touched something warm and alive. I drew my hand back and looked up. On the wall of the cave was a beautiful quartz crystal, its brilliant glow showing me the way forward. I looked closely and yes, there were rainbows and a miniature city bustling with activity.

I knew that my destiny was set. My reality is what I make it and my journey is to share my experiences with others, so that they too may awaken to the wonders of life.

Thank you to all of my new friends – I'll see you in my dreams.

Other titles by Jude Downes

From Grief to Goddess Book and Healing Cards
2014 self-published by Jude Downes and Animal Dreaming Publishing

Gateway to the Modern Crone
2019 self-published by Jude Downes and Adala Publishing

The Story of Woman The Mountain
Book One
2019 self-published by Jude Downes and Adala Publishing

Rise of the Wise Woman
2019 self-published by Jude Downes and Adala Publishing

www.ingramcontent.com/pod-product-compliance
Lightning Source LLC
Chambersburg PA
CBHW070615120726
47909CB00004B/1223